LIANA

KATHRYN J. BAIRD

LIANA

TATE PUBLISHING
AND ENTERPRISES, LLC

Liana

Published by Tate Publishing & Enterprises, LLC
127 E. Trade Center Terrace | Mustang, Oklahoma 73064 USA
1.888.361.9473 | www.tatepublishing.com

Tate Publishing is committed to excellence in the publishing industry. The company reflects the philosophy established by the founders, based on Psalm 68:11,
"The Lord gave the word and great was the company of those who published it."

Cover design by Rtor Maghuyop
Interior design by Jimmy Sevilleno

Published in the United States of America

ISBN: 978-1-68028-388-4
Fiction / Christian / General
15.02.13

IN MEMORY OF MY BELOVED
MOTHER
GARNETT BAUGH

1

LIANA WAS HOME alone when the earthquake shattered her world. The entire house was knocked high off the ground and then it came crashing down. She froze with fear from the deafening roar of furniture and household items colliding. The sofa Liana was on slid across the hardwood floor smashing into the wall. 'This is the real thing' she thought, knowing in her heart it was bad. The ceiling in the middle of the room and some rafters caved in, if the sofa had not moved it would have fallen on Liana and probably have killed her. Moving as fast as she could, Liana got out of the sofa and turned it over, just as she got under it, the sofa slid back to the middle of the floor. It didn't go far before it hit all the rubble. She was frantic and began praying, screaming her prayers to God.

"Please Lord, keep me and my family safe, put your hand on us and keep us safe from any harm."

She continued praying for her mother, father, brother and sister. It sounded like everything was being ripped and torn apart, she could feel it when the roof gave in. The sofa came down on her, but fortunately didn't cave completely in; she was in really close quarters now. The rumble seemed to go on forever, when it finally stopped she was crying hysterically, calling out to God over and over.

Liana lay there quietly, listening intently, she heard nothing. Every once in a while she would hear a board or something fall. She tried to push herself up, but the sofa wouldn't budge. She was lying on her stomach and couldn't move the sofa. Liana thought if she could get on her back perhaps she could push with her feet. She struggled to turn over, but was unable to pull her legs up to get her feet on the sofa. She lay there for hours, praying most of the time. Liana wasn't too worried about her family, they had gone to a sale barn about fifty miles east of where they lived, to buy some cattle. After laying there for hours, she finally drifted off to sleep.

Liana was raised on a cattle ranch just outside of Sana Cruz, Ca. She and her brother Alex and her sister Bella had been home schooled all their lives. Now that she was 18, Liana was getting ready to go to Venezuela to work with her aunt and uncle in their orphanage. Her brother Alex was 16 and her sister was now 14 years old. Their parents

Emily and Dan had raised them in a Christian home and taught them to work on the ranch. Liana was a beautiful girl with dark hair and her eyes were stunning. When she was in a room, all eyes were drawn to her. Her sister was beautiful like her and her brother very handsome. People always told their parents what a lovely family they were.

Something awakened Liana, it took her a minute to figure out where she was. The panic returned.

"Is anybody here?" She heard a man yelling.

"Help me!" She screamed, "I'm here, I'm here."

She heard things being moved.

"Are you under the sofa?"

"Yes, help me."

"I am trying to get to you," he said with a grunt, shoving a beam out of the way.

Finally the sofa was lifted just enough for her to crawl out.

"Oh, thank God, I didn't know if anybody would ever find me."

"Listen, we need to find a safe place before the aftershock hits, at least we need to get out of here," his voice sounded urgent.

He grabbed her hand and pulled her toward the outside, going through a hole in the wall. Liana was aghast when she saw the devastation.

"What are we going to do?" She questioned.

They were running up a hill and before he could answer, the earthquake erupted again.

The earth shook and threw them to the ground, they grabbed each other and held tight. The ground they were lying on was pushed upward toward the sky and it began falling out from under him. He rolled over on her to keep from falling into a deep crevice. Before the land they were lying on fell from beneath them, the eruption stopped.

They were lying on a small piece of ground protruding in the air. The ground the house was on was gone and all around them was water. They were on the only piece of land still above water. As far as they could see was water.

The water had debris floating everywhere.

"If there is another aftershock, we won't make it. We need to grab some of this lumber floating around and try to prepare it so we can float on it. Can you swim?"

"Yes," she said quietly.

He could tell she was in shock, "Hey, if we are going to make it you are going to have to be very brave. I can tell you are in shock, but you have to help me."

She was staring straight ahead, he took her chin and turned her head toward him, "Can you be brave."

She didn't answer, he shook her head lightly, "I said can you be brave," he said loudly.

She looked at him, "I'm so scared, are we going to die?"

She began to cry.

"Not if you can calm down and help me. Do you want to die?"

"No," she said as she lifted her chin.

"Okay then, let's find something we can float on."

Liana started praying to herself saying 'please God let us find something, please save us.'

"Look," she yelled, "what is that thing?"

He saw it at the same time she did, "It looks like a small deck or something."

He jumped into the water and swam to it, grabbing hold he pulled it toward Liana. When he got close enough, she took hold of it. He got out of the water and pulled it onto the land. It was a small deck with rails, he looked it over wondering if they could trust their lives on this thing. He could tell somebody really put it together good.

"Looks like we will have to take a chance on this if another aftershock happens," she said.

"Yeah, the water is going to get really rough, but this looks pretty sturdy," he answered.

They sat on their little piece of land hoping rescue would come. There had not been any sightings of helicopters or any other form of rescue. They were both very quiet. Neither of them could believe what they were seeing.

"Looks like this is the big one they always said was coming, where California falls off into the sea. I wonder how much of Santa Cruz got it. I've read a little of the San Andreas Fault and the really knowledgeable seismologists have always said there's no way this could happen, they always said it was impossible," he told her.

"From the looks of things, they were wrong."

Off in the distance, Liana could see something, "What is that?" She asked nervously.

They watched as it got closer, "Oh my god, it looks like a big wave, get into the raft."

They quickly climbed into the platform with railings. By the time the wave got to them it was much smaller, but was so forceful they felt like they were flying through the air. Liana was lying on the floor and hanging onto the deck as tight as she could. The water was rushing over her and when she couldn't hold her breath any longer, the wave quit flowing over them and started pulling them the other way. They were moving fast, back out into the open sea.

Other debris had been banging into them and some of the railings were knocked off, other than that their little platform held together very well. They floated for about an hour before the sun began to set.

They talked for a while, she told him her name and he said his name was Nicholas Reeves and that he was from Hollywood, Ca.

She giggled when he said Hollywood and said, "Really, you live in Hollywood?"

"Yes," he smiled, "I grew up there."

"Wow, what is that like?"

"I like it there," he answered, then said, "I was out riding my horse when this happened."

"Do you keep your horse stabled out here somewhere?"

"Yes," he said again, "Do you know where the Weathersby Stables are?"

"Why yes," she told him, "That's right next to our ranch."

"I've ridden around your ranch lots of times."

The night was pitch black, Liana had her arms wrapped around herself, she was beginning to get cold.

"We better set next to each other for body heat, it always gets pretty cool at night out here, especially when you're wet."

He moved over and put his arm around her, Liana felt funny, she had never had a man, except her dad or brother, put his arm around her. She blushed, she was glad it was dark so he couldn't see her.

She cleared her voice and said, "You sound like you've been out here a lot at night."

"Yeah, I have a sailboat I keep in Santa Cruz."

The sun was just beginning to rise when Liana awoke. They were laying on their raft cuddled up together, he had his arms around her and was holding her tight. She moved quickly out of his arms. He rolled over into a fetal position and continued sleeping.

Liana got her first really good look at him. She thought him to be very handsome, probably the best looking man she had ever seen. He had dark thick hair a little longer than most men and as he woke up, she saw how truly beautiful his eyes were.

"Good morning," he said, then grinning he continued, "this is the hardest bed I have ever slept on."

"I agree," she smiled.

They floated and talked throughout the day. She asked him what he did and when he told her he was an actor, he couldn't believe she had never heard of him.

"Don't you ever go to the movies? " He asked.

"No, we don't have a TV either," she offered.

"Are you serious?" He questioned.

"No, my parent's homeschooled us.

"What on earth do you do?"

"We do lots of things, probably even more than most families do. We have our church family and run the ranch, which I love and, of course, homeschool. We go on lots of vacations, skiing, boating and we do a lot of camping, I love my life."

"I can't imagine a life without TV or movies, so you've really never heard of me."

"No, but I think you are probably a very good actor."

"I'm the highest paid actor in the business right now, I'm not bragging, it's a fact. So that does make me the best in the business," he said proudly.

"Wow," she said.

She lay down on her stomach and put her head on her arms and closed her eyes. Nicholas was looking at her, he could see how attractive her darker skin and black hair was. With her eyes closed he could see how black and long her lashes were. He could tell she didn't wear make-up and was naturally beautiful without it. Most of the women he knew were always made up and beautiful, it was nice meeting a girl who didn't need all that.

They floated for three more days, their raft was always moving very fast, it was never just slowly floating in the water. Nicholas thought it was because of the earthquake, he said the earthquake probably has caused wave after wave in the ocean.

"I don't know how far we have gone, but we are a long way from home," he said.

"We have really been moving fast this whole time," she said worriedly. "We could be hundreds of miles out."

"I hope we bump into an island soon," he told her jokingly.

He knew if they didn't find land soon that they would perish. Nicholas didn't tell Liana that, he always tried to comfort her. Every night they lay in each other's arms, he liked holding her. She felt funny about it, but knew it was only for survival. They talked about their lives, she told him about her family, he could tell she came from people totally different from his. He knew she was a Christian and very strong in her faith. He had been in show business since he was a little boy and never had an ordinary life. He had been to church a few times, but thought it was all foolishness. She couldn't believe it when she found out he didn't believe in God. He had everything he could ever want in life so why did he need God. He knew she would be shocked if she really knew the way he lived. Always partying, never settling for one woman. He liked her, but knew she had no interest in him. This was something very new to him, he could always have any woman he wanted. He had never been with a woman who hadn't flirted and thrown herself at him.

Every day, they watched for land and each day they got weaker and more dehydrated. Once she asked him how long a person could go without water, he told her he didn't know, but probably not more than a week. He knew that most people perish much sooner than that, but didn't want to tell her that. They were badly sunburned by now and their lips were blisters.

Liana said her prayers silently every night. On the fifth night he knew they probably wouldn't make it till morning. They had been without water to long, she knew it too, but neither of them said anything. After they lay down, he knew she was praying.

"Hey, why don't you pray out loud, I'd like to hear you?"

Liana was used to praying out loud with her family and friends and at first she was a little shy about praying in front of him, knowing he didn't believe.

She began to pray, "Dear Father God, I thank you for everything, and I'm asking you for your protection for Nicholas and me. I know our lives are in your hands and I pray you will save us from this sea. Please we need food, water and shelter. I pray you won't let us perish. I pray especially that you won't let Nicholas perish before he turns to you in his life and accepts Jesus Christ as his Lord and savior. If I die, I know where I'll be, I'll be with you Lord, but I'm asking you to please save Nicholas. And I pray dear Lord that you will be with all those who have lost loved ones in this earthquake and I ask you to protect my family and pray that I will see them again. I pray in Jesus Holy name. Amen.

"Wow," he said and hugged her. "If we live it will be your faith that saved us."

2

THEY WERE AWAKENED the next morning by the sound of very loud splashing water. When Nicholas looked up he could see an island. It wasn't very big he could see from one end of it to the other, maybe a couple of miles. When they got closer to shore, they were moving very quickly, Nicholas grabbed Liana with one arm and held the railing with the other. He could tell they were going much too fast as they hit the rocks, the raft flew into the air and both Liana and Nicholas were thrown out.

Nicholas' leg was cut very badly by some sharp rocks, Liana was unhurt.

Liana ran to Nicholas when she saw his leg, she knew it was bad.

"Help me up," he grimaced.

She put his arm around her neck and pulled him up. She held him as he hobbled out of the rocks and onto shore. There was a small sandy beach, she helped him sit down then pulled her t-shirt off and tore a long strip around the bottom of it. She wrapped it tightly around his cut to stop the bleeding. Then she put what was left of her t- shirt back on. The blood soaked through the cloth, but stopped pretty quickly.

"We have to find water as soon as we can," she said, "but, first I will try to find a shady spot for you. You're in no shape to walk looking for water, I'll be right back."

She headed towards the vegetation, not far from where Nicholas was she found some small trees with enough shade to put him under while she looked for water. Once he was comfortable Liana headed into the island. Her family often camped out and she was not at all nervous. When she had walked nearly a mile Liana heard a loud noise that sounded like rushing water. She began to run toward the sound, her heart accelerated when she saw the waterfall. When she reached the water, she looked up at the waterfall it was beautiful. Liana walked right into the pool of water and drank her fill. It was wonderful, she knew the only way to get water to Nicholas was to bring him to it. She ran most of the way back.

"I found water," she said excitedly.

Liana could see the relief on Nicholas' face, he tried to smile and said, "I knew your faith would save us."

Liana helped him up and practically carried him to the waterfall. Having grown up on the ranch and doing hard work most of her life had made her very strong for a girl. She helped him to walk into the pool of water and watched as he drank his fill. While he was drinking she looked around for a place for them to camp. She spotted what looked like a cave in some rocks on the other side of the pool.

"Look is that a cave over there?" She asked.

Nicholas looked where she pointed, "I don't believe it, it looks like a cave to me, let's walk over there and see."

"No you sit down here by the water and I'll go over there, no need in you walking over there with your leg the way it is, if it's not a cave."

She went to the other side and found a cave in the rocks, it was big enough to stand up in and had a dirt floor. Liana went outside and waved to Nicholas and yelled it's a cave. Then she went back and helped him to the other side. The sun was shining and they decided to stay outside until their clothes dried. Liana started looking at limbs of trees.

"What are you looking for?" He asked.

"You aren't going to believe this, but my brother and I used to spear fish all the time when we went camping. I saw lots of fish in the shallow part of the pool. If I can find a good limb and sharpen it maybe I can get a fish."

He laughed and said, "I'm sure glad I got into this mess with you instead of some sissy girl who couldn't do anything."

Liana found a branch and said, "Watch this," the way she tore it off the limb caused it to have a sharp end on it.

Nicholas was impressed, "Wow, how'd you learn that?"

"I and my brother learned how to do that years ago, when we went camping we were always trying survival skills." she said with a smile.

She walked to the pool and stood there watching, then she waded out about knee deep and stood there for a while. She moved slowly around the pool looking with the spear held up ready to strike. Swiftly she thrust the spear into the water, coming up with a fish on it.

Liana screamed and laughed saying, "My first try!" She was joyous.

She ran up to Nicholas and showed him the fish, he was laughing hardily.

"Now, how do you propose to cook it?"

"Well, my brother and I also learned how to start fires with sticks."

"You're kidding?"

"No," she said laughing as she started looking for what she called good sticks for a fire.

It took a while, but she finally found sticks she thought would work. He sat up watching her. The bottom stick was wide and dry and had a crack in it, she laid it on the ground and put a small pile of dried brush up around it and taking a small thinner stick she put the end of it in the crack on the stick on the ground and started rubbing her hands back and forth on the stick she was holding. Eventually she got some sparks going on the brush and very carefully blew on it and added more brush, the brush began to flame and she added more. When Liana had a nice fire going she looked at Nicholas and smiled proudly.

"Wow, I can't believe it, you prayed for food, water and shelter and we got shelter and food and water," he said in amazement.

"God is good," she said without any doubt.

She speared two more fish then put them on the fire. When they were eating the fish Nicholas said it was the best thing he had ever eaten, they laughed. Both were completely relieved knowing they were going to live. The happiness showed in both of them, they teased each other and talked and laughed until dark.

The dirt floor in the cave felt a little better than the raft. It was dark inside, she set down and he set next to her, he put his arm around her and turned her toward him and started to kiss her. Liana was surprised and without thinking she shoved him violently away.

"What are you doing," she said in terror, as she got to her feet.

"I was going to kiss you, I thought you liked me," he answered in confusion.

"How dare you, you may act this way with other women, but when God sends my mate, I plan on being innocent and go to him pure. I have prayed for a mate most of my life and he will be a good Godly man as pure as I am and he will love God as much as I do."

He was still lying on the cave floor where she had shoved him. He was totally surprised, that was the first time a woman had ever refused him.

"Wow," he said, "I am very sorry, please don't be mad at me, I just thought you liked me, we were having such a good time."

"That still doesn't give you the right to disrespect me like that."

"Don't worry, I won't do it again," he said angrily.

Nicholas stood up and hobbled out of the cave.

Liana was stunned, she thought she shouldn't have been so mean, 'but, how dare him,' she thought. It took her hours to go to sleep, she heard him come in and move to the other side of the cave.

Something caused her a wake early in the morning, it was Nicholas groaning. Liana went to where he lay. She could tell he was sick, she felt his forehead and he was burning up with a very high fever. Liana was very alarmed, she knew it was probably infection in his leg, she took the rag off the gash below his knee. Infection was oozing out of it, she ran to the pool of water, taking her t-shirt off as she ran. Washing it in the water as good as she could, she wrung it out and ran back to the cave. Using the t-shirt she cleaned the wound as good as she could then went back to the water and rinsed out the t-shirt and took it back to wipe his sweat covered face. While she was cleaning his face he came to, looking at her in confusion.

"You're very sick Nicholas," she said, "Your leg is badly infected.

Tears started down her face, "Don't worry," he said, "I'm to mean to die."

"No you're not mean," she said, "I'm the mean one, I shouldn't have talked to you the way I did yesterday, I'm so sorry."

"It's okay, it's kind of refreshing knowing there's a woman in this world with morals and will stand up for herself. I'm the one that should tell you I'm sorry, when I thought about it later, I realized how disrespectful that really was. I was going to apologize to you today."

"You don't need to apologize, we're good," she said smiling, "and I do like you."

Then he grinned, "Is there any hope for me then?"

"If you're talking about kissing than the answer is no," she smiled.

"What about if I ask you very respectfully some time for a kiss," he said teasingly.

She blushed.

Then he added in a surprised tone, "You've never been kissed have you?"

"Yes I have," she said defiantly.

"I mean by a man."

She blushed again, "Yes I have."

"Oh, that poor guy, I bet when you slapped him and his face stayed red for days," he said laughing.

"Yes, and he deserved it," she said stubbornly.

He laughed out loud as if it were the funniest thing he ever heard. She couldn't help it and started laughing too.

Then he grabbed his leg in pain, "This leg is killing me."

"It really looks bad, I wish we had some antibiotics, I'm going to go find something to eat, you rest and I'll be right back."

She went back to where she had picked berries yesterday and picked more. When she returned he was sleeping so she didn't disturb him. Setting beside him she lay her hands on his shoulder and began praying. She asked God to heal him and not let him die and lead him to salvation.

He woke up when she touched him, but lay there quietly listening to her prayer. He realized he was actually thankful for her praying for him. He was so sick and for some reason he believed her prayers had saved them and somehow knew this prayer she prayed for him would ultimately heal him. He wondered if he could believe in a God like she did. He thought about how good it would be to have a God to help you and lean on when you needed him. Nicholas had never really been around anyone like Liana before. Maybe he was wrong maybe there is a God and he has lived without him all his life. Then he started thinking about the life he has lived and knew that God would never accept him. Disappointed in his thoughts, he drifted off to sleep.

Nicholas ran a high temperature for three days, Liana knew it was terribly high. She prayed often over him. She would take her t-shirt and get it wet and carry it back and squeeze water into his mouth and then wipe his face and arms trying to get the fever down. She didn't know what would happen without antibiotics and was very scared.

On the fourth day she felt something on her nose. Upon opening her eyes, she saw Nicholas was setting by her with a leaf tickling her.

She sat up and smiled, "So, you were to mean to die."

He laughed, "Last night I woke up drenched in sweat, I guess the fever broke and I tell you, I feel one hundred percent better," he pulled his pant leg up and continued, "Look my leg is scabbed over a little and healing."

"Thank you God," she said, praising the Lord.

"Amen," he said earnestly, "I told you your faith would save us, I heard you pray for me a lot while I was sick and I thank you for that."

"You need to thank God not me, there was nothing I could do."

He looked up and said, "Thank you Lord for healing me and saving us."

A little embarrassed he then said, "Hey, I'm ready for a good swim or maybe just a dog paddle so I can get this sweat washed off me, would you like to join me."

Liana laughed, "I would love to sir."

The water was refreshing, she splashed him and swam away.

"Hey just wait till I get my strength back, paybacks are painful."

"I'm hungry," she said, "I think I'll scrounge up some breakfast."

He watched her graceful body move away, Nicholas had never met anybody like her before. He knew he was beginning to like her a lot, but knew he didn't have a chance with her. She's looking for a man who grew up knowing God, a true Christian. He wished he had paid attention the few times he went to church. He really knew nothing of the bible.

After breakfast he asked her to tell him about salvation, he said he knew the stories about Jesus, how he was born of a virgin and was God's son. But he had never read the bible and knew nothing about it. So Liana told him about Jesus and the disciples and how Jesus taught them. For several days they ate, swam and she told him mostly the stories in the bible that centered on Jesus and salvation.

One morning he told her he was feeling much better and would like to explore the island. She had actually been over most of it, but she was glad to go with him. He told her he thought they should make something that would catch the eye of a plane flying over. The whole time they had been there only a couple of planes flew over and they were too high to see them.

"What about going up on the mountain where the waterfall is and maybe using some rocks to spell out SOS, or doing the same with dark rocks down on the beach."

"That could work, let's climb that mountain and see what it looks like up there."

Because of all the brush, climbing up above the waterfall was impossible, so they headed for the beach. The beach ran about a quarter of a mile, but wasn't real wide. They decided to put an SOS sign on it and began looking for dark colored rocks. Luckily, there were lots of rocks not far off the beach. They spent about three hours carrying rocks before they had the three letters spelled out. When they finished they stood back and looked at their work.

"I think it will work," he said.

"Yeah, the letters are big enough for a plane flying pretty high to read them." She answered.

They were hot and sweaty and when they returned to the waterfall they went into the water to cool off. She floated on her back and he stood watching her, he thought she was perfect in every way and knew he would never be satisfied with any of the women he used to be with. They were all glitz and glamour and very beautiful, but very shallow and most of them wanted to be with him because of his fame.

That night Liana began to cough, as the night progressed she coughed more and more. In the morning she woke feeling terrible.

"Oh no," she said, "I think I have a cold."

"Yes, I heard you coughing most of the night."

"Usually when I get a cold I get strip throat and have to have an antibiotic. Growing up I got sick sometimes twice a month and had to have antibiotics. I actually needed my tonsils out, but my pediatrician wouldn't let me have the surgery because a patient of his, a small boy died on the operating table and after that he always just treated tonsillitis with antibiotics. Now when I get a cold it usually ends up to be tonsillitis and I get really sick. I hope that doesn't happen this time, I can't stand it."

"Why don't you get your tonsils out now?"

"I haven't been sick for quite some time now, but I know I should, I just haven't done it yet."

That night she became sicker and started running a fever, he woke up and went over to check on her, when he touched her forehead, he could tell she had a fever. Nicholas took his shirt off and went to the pool and rinsed it out then wrung it out and took it back to wipe her face and lay it on her forehead to try to get the fever down. He had heard somewhere if you cool off the joints in the body like the bend inside the elbow it would also keep the fever down. He would move the shirt from her forehead to the arms trying to cool her down. It seemed to work she seemed not to be as hot. Finally she started sleeping more peacefully.

The next day she had a fever all day, but she was able to go to the pool to drink water. That night it got worse, she started shivering uncontrollably, he lay beside her and held her in his arms trying to warm her. She started talking out of her mind, mumbling things he couldn't understand, then it struck him, 'maybe she's praying' he thought.

"It's okay Liana," he whispered in her ear, "I'll pray for you. Please Lord Help Liana she needs you now, please heal her quickly."

He continued to hold her and pray quietly to her the rest of the night. At dawn she quit shivering and fell very quiet. He lay her down and looked at her, fear went through him.

"Liana," he shook her lightly, "Liana wake up."

She didn't move, he tried several times to wake her but she did not respond. Her body was burning up and he knew she was in real danger. He had to get the fever down. Nicholas picked her up and carried her to the pool. He walked into it to his waist and lowered her a little into the water. Very slowly he lowered her a little more, after a few minutes he carried her back to the cave. Nicholas sat on the floor, leaning against the wall with her in his lap and her head laying against his chest. He was so afraid. He began to pray and cry, begging God to save her, pleading with God. He promised God that if he let her live that he would change his life and live the way God wanted him to. Eventually he quit crying and fell asleep.

3

When Nicholas awoke he was still holding Liana, she was lifeless, fear shot through his body. He gently laid her down, she was breathing, he shook her, but she did not respond. He opened her eyelid, nothing, no movement.

"Please God," he cried out, "You are the only one that can help her, she loves you so much, please don't let her die."

Nicholas had never been this helpless or frightened in his life. He felt of her forehead, she had no temperature.

'Then what happened,' he thought. He took his t-shirt and went to the pool, there he rinsed it as good as he could and took it back wringing wet. He twisted it and put the end of it in her mouth, squeezing it, he could tell water was going into her mouth then he saw her swallow. He gave her several drinks then wiped her face.

He sat by her for hours watching for some kind of movement, she was completely still. Several times he gave her water. By afternoon he was completely exhausted from worry and fell asleep. They both slept the rest of the day and through the night. He awoke at dawn the light was just coming into the cave. Nicholas was astounded that he slept so long, he went quickly over to Liana and she seemed to be sleeping peacefully. He felt her forehead and at his touch, she awakened.

It was the happiest he had ever been, "How are you?" He asked.

"I'm hungry," she said, "I woke up last night, but you were asleep then I went back to sleep."

"I thought you were going to die, I was so afraid."

"I know the feeling, when you were sick, I thought you were going to die to."

He looked at her and kissed her on the forehead, "God is good, I prayed for you and He answered my prayer."

"Oh, Nicholas that's wonderful," she set up and hugged him.

"When you get better, you will have to tell me what to do to get saved."

"Oh no, we mustn't wait, if you love God and believe in Him then you must get saved now."

"What should I do?"

"Well, let me just ask you, do you believe that God is a living God and that Jesus is his son who came to earth as a man and died on the cross taking all our sins then rose again on the third day and ascended into heaven. And is now setting at the right hand side of God the Father in heaven. And do you believe that you are a sinner and will you repent from your sins?"

"I do believe that now, I have no doubt there is a God. First he saved us from the earthquake that we both should have died in. I mean the only piece of land left was the land we were on. Then He gave us the perfect raft. While on the raft you prayed and He put us on this island with food and shelter. After that I got sick and your prayers saved my life. Then you got sick and I finally truly turned to God. All of these things were life and death situations and you or I could not save us, it was absolutely miracles from God that we have lived. I don't need anything else to happen to make me believe. I have no doubts this all came from God."

Liana began to cry, she put her face in her hands and cried.

"Why are you crying?" He said as he moved over by her and put his arm around her, "Hey, its okay."

"I'm just so happy," she said as she continued crying, "I've never been this happy."

"I'm happy to," he told her as he pulled her to him and held her tight.

Liana was still crying when she said, "I'm still hungry to."

He started laughing, "Oh, you poor thing, I'm sorry, I'll be right back."

When he was gone Liana lay back down and told God how thankful she was. She was ecstatic and if she felt better she was sure she would be dancing around.

Nicholas wished he could get her something better than berries but he had no skills to kill animals. He decided to have Liana teach him how to spear. She had speared a rabbit a while back and it was delicious. He also wished they had a pot to cook in.

The next couple of weeks Nicholas kept Liana telling him about the bible, she told him the Old Testament. He understood how it leads to Jesus and how close those people were to God. Liana knew every book in the bible and told him each one as well as she could. She explained Revelations and told him about the tribulations.

"The tribulations are going to be hard to live through," he said.

She then told him about what Christians called the Rapture, she said she didn't think Christians would have to live through the tribulations that she believed God would take them home before the tribulations happened. She explained that some Christians believed they would be raptured out mid-tribulations and others believed it would be after. But, she believed it would be before.

"You mean it's not black and white that nobody really knows."

"No the bible isn't always black and white to us, I'm sure it is to God though."

"I wish I had a bible so I could study it, when we get back, that's the second thing I'm getting. The first thing is a big steak dinner for us."

Liana laughed, "Sounds great."

Liana taught him how to hunt with a spear. He practiced for hours sometimes. Finally one day he was out hunting when he actually speared a rabbit. Nicholas brought it back with a big grin on his face.

"Bravo!"

"Now you are going to have to show me how to skin it."

She showed him how to pull the skin off the rabbit in one piece. That night, they enjoyed the meat so much, neither of them could quit talking about how good it was. He told her his rabbit was better than hers. They argued teasingly with each other for a while then decided to take a swim. In the pool he got hold of her and ducked her. Still holding her with a firm grip he brought her head out of the water and asked if paybacks were painful. She refused to give in and told him no. He ducked her again and pulled her up.

"Do you give up now?"

"No."

He said, "You are the most stubborn person I have ever met."

He let her go and she splashed him good then ran out of the pool. He chased her and finally caught her. Grabbing her around the waist, they both went down, they lay on their backs and laughed.

"Then he turned on his side and looked at her, "Tell me, if I asked for a kiss now, would you give me one?"

She jumped up and started running, "Only if you can catch me."

By the time he caught her they were both out of breath, "All right, you owe me a kiss, but you will have to wait till I catch my breath."

No, it has to be right now."

He looked at her and kissed her lips, it was a short sweet kiss, but it was magical. He had never felt this way from kissing a girl before. Her heart was pounding, she was sure he could feel it. She was blushing when she pushed him away.

"There now," he said, "you've had your first kiss, are you blushing?"

She blushed more, "You are blushing," he teased.

That night the only thing either of them could think of was the kiss.

She couldn't believe how wonderful it was. She was so happy, but knew she shouldn't be. She knew when they were rescued that he would go back to his life. She knew he could have any woman in the world and the only reason he was giving her any attention was because they were stuck here together. If they had met any other time, he would not have given her a second look. She knew he couldn't possibly love her. She was nobody and he was a great actor, but she would cherish the kiss forever.

He also knew she couldn't possibly love him. The life he lived was so sinful and she had even said the mate God gave her would be pure. He was far from pure, if he had only known God when he was a boy and grew up learning the right way to live. Well, it was too late now he supposed. At least he has these great memories of her. After they are rescued he didn't think she would ever see him again.

They had been on the island for two months, their clothes were worn thin and they had lost so much weight that the clothes hung on them. They stayed busy each day looking for food. One day she watched him as he speared a fish, he was so handsome, and she knew she was really falling for him, but also knew she shouldn't. She refused to let herself dwell on how much she liked him. Liana knew when they got back that she would probably never see him again. She would become very sad about that and one day when she was being depressed about it he came up.

"What's wrong you look very blue?"

"I was just thinking about leaving this island, I have learned to love it here and I am going to miss it. And, when we get back we will probably never see each other again and that makes me sad."

"Why wouldn't we see each other again?"

"Well, you're famous and will be going back to your life and will be very busy."

"Liana, you have become one of my very best friends, I hope we will see each other a lot. I have never had such a good time trying to survive," he smiled.

The next day they both heard the helicopter at the same time, it had landed on the beach. They looked at each other and started running toward the beach yelling. When they reached the helicopter they asked the pilot how he found them. He said an airplane had flown over this morning and seen their SOS. They contacted the Coast Guard and the Coast Guard sent them out.

"Get in," he said with a smile, "You're going home."

They got in and when the pilot looked at him, he said, "Hey, are you Nicholas Reeves?"

"The very same," Nicholas said.

"Wow, they thought you were killed in the earthquake, I think I'll radio ahead and tell them that you have been found."

The pilot asked Liana her name then got on the radio and told them he had Nicholas Reeves and Liana Baugh in his chopper. By the time they landed in San Francisco the media was already there waiting for them. They walked out on the tarmac and the media immediately rushed at Nicholas.

"Wait a minute, wait a minute," Nicholas said sternly to them, "Let me take care of Liana here and get settled somewhere and my agent can talk to you. I am not going to talk to you right now."

"But Nicholas," one reporter yelled, "How did you end up on that island with such a pretty girl."

The photographers were taking hundreds of pictures.

Liana could sense that Nicholas was angry.

He turned to the reporter and grabbed him by his collar, "What do you not understand about I'm not talking to you now?" He shoved the guy back and looked fiercely at the other reporters, "Now get out of our way."

He grabbed Liana's hand and pulled her away from the crowd. A member of the Coast Guard came up to them and asked them to go with him.

In the Coast Guard quarters, they were taken to a nicely decorated room with some sofas in it. A high ranking officer was waiting for them.

"Mr. Reeves we have notified your agent and he is on his way and we also were able to reach Ms. Baugh's family, they are also coming. It could be a couple of hours before they get here is there anything we can get for you."

Nicholas looked at Liana then said, "Is it possible to get a steak dinner, we haven't eaten much except berries and fish for quite some time now, however, we did have a couple of rabbits."

"We have a mess hall and I'm sure the cook can fix you some steak."

"Can you bring the chef to us please, I don't think we're in the mood for a mess hall."

"Certainly, the entire Coast Guard is at your service. Anything you would like we will find a way to get it for you."

"I think just a steak."

"What about some other clothing?"

"No," he said, "We're fine thank you."

The officer left and Nicholas said, "I hope you don't care about changing clothes, but I would like our last day together to be the way we are now. I have too many good memories of us just the way we are."

She laughed, "Our shorts are dirty, and our t-shirts are rags."

"Yes, I know and nobody else in the world could make those rags look so good."

She blushed again, "I love it when you blush and I have never known any girl that blushed before."

"Well, I hate it," she said. "It's embarrassing."

While they were talking, the chef came in, "What would you like with your steak and how do you like your steak? I'll be famous when people find out I cooked for Nicholas Reeves," he said while laughing.

Then he continued, "Seriously though, I'm very happy that you lived through all you have been through and would truly like to make your first meal back as pleasing as I can."

He told them all the side dishes that were available and took their order, in the meantime a waiter came with ice water and iced tea. He also brought homemade rolls and butter.

"Maybe we shouldn't eat too much bread before our meal gets here, I'd hate to get to full to eat the steak." She advised.

"You're probably right, but oh, it tastes so good."

Their food arrived and they ate hardily, they both had to quit before they were even half way through.

Oh," Nicholas complained, "I ate too much."

She couldn't help laughing, "I know, me to."

At that time the door opened and Liana's parents and brother and sister came in. When she saw them she got up and ran to them. They all wrapped their arms around her, hugging her and laughing and crying.

"We thought you were dead," her dad said wiping tears from his eyes, "We can't believe that you are alive. I told them if anybody could survive that, Liana could."

Then her mother said, "We're so happy Liana, we have never been this happy in our lives."

"Are you ready to go, we can't wait to hear your story," her brother said.

"Wait a minute," her dad said, "Let's meet this man that helped her all this time, I'm sure God sent him so you wouldn't be alone."

Liana brought her family over to meet Nicholas, they didn't know he was an actor, actually they didn't' know anything about him. They had just found out that they were alive.

Liana introduced them to Nicholas, her father thanked him for helping Liana and being with her the entire time.

Her dad said, "I never quit praying for Liana and in all my prayers, I asked God that if she was still alive, that somebody was with her helping her."

Nicholas smiled and said, "In all actuality Liana was the one that helped me, if not for her, I probably would not have made it. She knows how to survive with a spear made from a tree limb and how to make a fire. Without her skills I'm sure I would have perished."

Liana's brother laughed, "That survival stuff finally came in handy did it?"

"Yes," Liana said, "You would have been proud of me, we had fish to eat and a couple of rabbits, one of them Nicholas speared."

"Well, there wasn't much to do on the island so I spent many days practicing, it took quite some time before I could spear a fish and a lot longer to spear the rabbit."

They all laughed then Liana's sister Bella said, "I know who you are, you're the famous actor."

"How did you know?" Liana asked.

"You mean you didn't, some of my friends used to talk about what great movies you make."

Liana looked at Nicholas and raising her eyebrows she said, "Well, the quite little sister knows more than her older sister."

Everybody laughed at that, then Nicholas said to Liana, "Before you go, May I have your phone number," then looking at her parents he said, "The experience we have been through together I'm sure has made us lifelong friends and I would like to keep in touch."

"Here, take one of my cards," her dad said, "It has our address and everything on it and I hope you will feel welcome to come to our place at any time."

"Thank you, I appreciate that invitation and the same goes for me, anytime you are in Hollywood please come by and see me. If you have another card I will write my address and phone number on it," looking over at Liana he continued as he wrote, "This is my personal phone and I am the only one that answers it." He handed the card to Liana.

While he was handing her the card someone shouted, "Nicholas!"

They looked over and a nice looking man came walking toward them. Nicholas went over and they hugged.

"I can't believe you survived all this time, we thought you had perished, you must have quite a story to tell."

"I do," Nicholas said grinning, then he turned and introduced his agent to the Baugh family, "This is my agent Robert Hamilton," he said then he introduced Liana and her family.

Robert looked at Liana and knew she was the person on the island with him, "I don't know how Nicholas gets so lucky, if I was stranded on an island I would never be so lucky to be stranded with such a pretty girl."

Liana blushed, Nicholas smiled at her and said, "I was lucky all right, if it hadn't been for her I would never have survived."

Then Liana's dad told them he was very happy to meet them, but he thought it was time to take his little girl home and take care of her.

They shook hands all around and headed in different directions.

4

ON THE WAY home all of Liana's family wanted to hear everything that happened to her, it was a two hour drive to where they lived now. Liana told them all that had happened, she told it like Nicholas talked about it. How God had saved them from the earthquake, and had given them a raft then the island and food and shelter. She talked about how he wanted to learn everything there was about God and how spending that much time on the island she was able to tell him everything she knew. She told them how he had gotten saved and then added that she thought it would have taken something like this experience to change him.

Liana's dad said, "God certainly worked in his life and there's no doubt God knew what He was doing."

"Yes," Liana agreed, "Now tell me about what happened with the earthquake, how bad was it."

Her mother said, "It was a strange earthquake, the worst of it was where our house was and the surrounding country. Santa Cruz got mostly water damage. Only you and Nicholas and two other people disappeared. Of course, we thought you were killed and now we find you alive, Praise God, so maybe the other two people are alive somewhere. It was an older man and woman, they owned Weathersby Stables."

"Oh no, that's where Nicholas kept his horse, he knew those people, I know that will break his heart, I'll call him when we get home."

Liana's dad's cell phone rang at that time, he handed the phone to Liana it was Nicholas.

"Hi," he said, "Just wanted to check on you and see how things are going. I heard about the earthquake only being where we were and hardly any damage in Santa Cruz. I was astounded, I was sure that earthquake was the big one."

"Me to," she answered, "I can't believe it was that small, I didn't think there would be anything left of Santa Cruz or any of the entire California coast line for that matter."

They laughed then he said, "I don't regret it happening, God changed my whole life. As a matter of fact, it was the best thing that has ever happened to me. I just told my agent that I would not do any more movies that didn't have wholesome Christian values. He's very unhappy with me right now, he says those kind of movies won't sell. He says only sex sells, but I'm going to prove him wrong. God gave me a talent and I am going to use it as a witness for Him."

"Oh, Nicholas that's wonderful, maybe if you make those kinds of movies all the Christians will be able to go to the theaters," she said happily.

Nicholas laughed, "Of course, then you can go see me act, but Liana, I hope you never see the movies I have done in the past. You or God certainly would not approve of them."

"Don't worry, you know all sins have been forgiven, past, present, and future."

"I know, but I regret making them, I shall spend my life making up for them."

Liana's parents were listening they both loved that Liana and Nicholas were talking about God.

"Liana," he said, "I do miss you already."

"I miss you too, we were together for such a long time and really under the circumstances we, at least I, enjoyed most of the time."

"Me to, it was wonderful, all we had was what was on our backs and it didn't matter, there was nothing pretentious about us."

"By the way, mom and Bella think you are a doll," Liana said teasingly.

"Well, you have me blushing now," he laughed.

"They want to know how old you are."

Bella was blushing now and said, "Liana don't tell him that."

Nicholas could hear Bella, he laughed, "It's okay," he said, "Tell her I'm 27 and I think she and your mother are dolls to."

Liana told them what he said and they laughed.

Liana's dad, Dan said to tell Nicholas that he had good taste. Liana told him and they were all laughing now.

"By the way, Liana, do you think you will have some spare time in a week or so? I'm going to read some movie scripts and I would like your opinion. Being such a new Christian, I don't want to make any mistakes and I value your opinion."

Liana's heart raced, "Sure, I'd be happy to, just call when you are ready to come."

"I will, in the meantime, I'm going to get this beard cut off and clean up, you probably won't recognize me when you see me. I'm going to see my father tonight, he is in a complete state of excitement, so I need to get there as quick as I can. I'll see you in a week or so."

"Yes," she said then added, "I already can't wait to see you."

"Me too, bye for now, I'll talk to you soon."

She told him bye and hung up.

Nicholas sat quietly for a while after talking to Liana.

His manager broke the silence, "I think you are sweet on that girl, she is very beautiful, you know the media will tear her apart. She's young and has never been chased by the media before. They took a lot of pictures of you guys and those pictures are going to come out in every magazine and tabloid and newspaper. I'm sure the news channels are already talking about your survival and the pretty young girl who survived with you."

"Your right, I never thought of that, I better call her back and warn them of the impending media rush that is about to turn their world upside down."

Liana answered the phone and was surprised that it was Nicholas, "Liana" he said, "I need to warn you about the media, they will probably drive you guys crazy, I'm sure they will find out where you live and impose on you and your family. The pictures they took of us will be all over the news and magazines and tabloids. They write anything that sells so they will probably make up stories about us. I just want you to be prepared, sometimes they get really ugly. Would you give the phone to your dad so I can talk to him about this, he may want to take extra precautions."

"Will it really be that bad? They don't even know me, here I'll let you talk to dad."

She handed the phone to her dad and Nicholas and he talked for a long time. Nicholas explained that because Liana was so pretty and young that the media might insinuate very hurtful things about her. He explained that he was known by the media as having a different woman with him all the time and they may put Liana into that category. He said he was sure all the reporters are going to want to know more about her and will probably drive them crazy.

Dan told him that they live in a pretty isolated area and in order for anyone to come to their ranch, they have to drive a half mile drive-way. He assured Nicholas that nobody could sneak around and get pictures without him knowing it. He said if they had any problems the sheriff would take care of it.

Then Dan said, "When you come to the ranch you'll see what I mean, if I have to I'll put one of the men who work for me on guard."

"That makes me feel much better, I do see you as a man who protects his family. I'm just sorry that knowing me will cause you this trouble."

"I'm not worried about what will happen because we know you. You mean a lot to us just for being there for Liana. You will always be a welcome guest to us."

"You may not feel that way after this media rush," Nicholas laughed, "You may want to kill me."

Dan laughed, "No, that won't happen I'm sure. Don't you worry about us?"

"Okay, well I'll see you in a week or two."

"That will be great," Dan said.

After hanging up, Dan told his family what Nicholas told him and they all talked about how they would handle it. Liana's mother, Emily thought that they should tell the media about Liana so they would know exactly what kind of person she is; instead of letting them write whatever they wanted. Her dad agreed and they decided that if the chance came they would invite some reporters in and talk to them.

When they finally reached their driveway, they saw that Nicholas was right. The media was there waiting at their gate. It was a big wrought iron gate with an automatic opener they used from their car. Liana's dad pulled up to the gate and stopped. He got out and asked them what was going on. The reporters moved in, there were about twenty of them, they had microphones and all their news vans were there. Several started talking at once, Dan put his hands in to air and told them he would be glad to talk to them.

When they were quiet he said, "But, let's go about this in a civilized way. As you know we thought our daughter was dead. We've just got her back today and we need to spend a little time together, let her relax at home and clean up. I think we need to take care of you men and women right away and without a doubt we need to talk to you so you won't write a bunch of nonsense about our daughter. Of course, we have never had any experience with the media, so we are going to go about this in the way we think most sensible. You want the news right now so we won't make you wait long. Just give us time to get ready for you and we will invite you in to our home and have a sit down talk."

The reporters were completely taken aback, they usually had to fight for a story and most people would not talk to them.

"Now we are going to open the gate and you may follow us in, you are invited to take pictures of the ranch while we are getting ready. This is the ranch we bought after ours was completely destroyed by the earthquake. Be careful around some of the horses, some are not friendly. I'm giving you the run of the place for a while so take all the pictures you want."

Several of the news people said thank you as the Baugh's entered the house.

Inside Alex started laughing, "Did you see the looks on their faces when dad didn't run them off."

"Yes," his mom said smiling, "I'm glad we decided what to do before we saw them, this could have turned out very differently."

"I'm going to take a wonderful bath and clean up, I can't wait to use shampoo on my hair. Where is my room?"

"Here I'll show you, "Bella volunteered.

On the way up the stairs Liana looked back and said, "By the way I love the house."

After her bath Liana put on some jeans and a pretty blue blouse, she couldn't believe how skinny she was, the jeans were way too big. She found Bella and asked if she had some jeans that might fit her. Bella found her some cute jeans, Liana put her favorite boots on and they felt funny after not having any shoes on for such a long time. When the earthquake happened she was barefoot and had been ever since. Nicholas had shoes on, but went barefoot most of the time, she thought it was because he felt guilty having shoes.

The family room was huge it had plenty of seating for the reporters. When Liana came downstairs, the reporters were already seated and were having coffee and tea. 'Leave it to mom,' she thought smiling to herself.

"Well, here she is now," Dan said. "We've been waiting for you and telling them all about our family. We've explained to them that we are devoted Christians and answered most of their questions about us. Now, they would like to ask you questions, do you feel like talking about this now."

"Yes," she said then looking around at the reporters she continued, "What would you like to know?"

One reporter asked her how it was to be stranded on the island with Nicholas.

"Actually, I was glad he was there it would have been a lot scarier if I was there by myself. Let me tell you all how everything happened."

She told them of the entire experience, about the earthquake and how Nicholas helped her out of the house and how the aftershock had lifted the land they were on and the raft, then the island with food, water and shelter. She told them how she had prayed and how God answered each prayer. She told them about him getting sick and her getting sick and how God had saved them and how it turned Nicholas into believing in God.

She talked for nearly two hours, they were amazed about her spear fishing and how they survived. She told them lots of funny stories, the reporters and her family were all glued to everything she said, they were loving it.

One reporter asked if she was in love with Nicholas, she blushed and said no, but she knew they would always be friends. That they had shared something very few people ever share and that their experience would bound them as friends forever.

After talking with Liana one reporter asked if they could take pictures of Liana and her family. Dan said they could and they took lots of pictures.

When they were done taking pictures each reporter respectfully shook hands with Liana and each one of her family. The reporters told them how refreshing it was to have met them and they were glad they knew the whole story and wouldn't have to speculate.

The reporters loved Liana and her family. When each of them got back to write their stories, they all wrote very complimentary things. One reporter compared her to Virgin Mary and talked about how Nicholas must have met his match, because he was unable to sweep her off her feet like he did most women. He talked about how she said her and Nicholas were friends for life and how lucky Nicholas was to have gained a friend like her.

The stories went on and on, one reporter wrote about how she saved Nicholas life with her survival skills and if she had not been there, he might not have made it.

The reporters that weren't at the interview picked up on the story in the same way and Liana became the darling of the media.

That night Liana lay in bed thinking about Nicholas, she thought he was probably with all of his friends celebrating his return. She knew that he could have any woman he wanted and she hated the thought that he might be with someone.

'This is silly,' she thought, 'I need to quit thinking about him, he is only a friend and I'm sure he is not even thinking about me now that he is back with his friends.' She rolled over and made her mind up not to think about him anymore. It still took her a long time to go to sleep.

The next day she was excited to be back home and couldn't wait to get back out with the animals. She was glad to find out that her horse had made it through the earthquake, but sad about all the animals that perished. She went out to the barn and saw that some raking was needed, she was raking the hay and manure out of some of the stalls when her dad came in.

"There you are, couldn't wait to get back to work?"

"Yeah," she said, "I have missed this so much. At least when we were on the island we were busy each day just trying to find something to eat. We didn't do very well though because I have lost twenty pounds, I have to wear Bella's clothes."

"Well, you'll get it back with your mothers cooking." They both laughed in agreement.

"Oh, dad," she said as she went and put her arms around him and laid her head on his shoulder. "I am so glad you guys were not here when this happened, the whole time I was gone I wasn't sure if you all were okay. I prayed a lot, but still didn't know. Nicholas and I really thought the earthquake was the big one and I was afraid that you might have been in it."

"I know how you felt, we didn't know if you were dead or alive, from the looks of it you were killed. We've looked for you the whole time you've been gone. We went through every crack and crevice. Some of the firemen actually took ropes and went down as far as they could looking for you. Of course, we didn't even know about Nicholas, well, we read his name many times in the paper and knew that a prominent actor had probably died in the earthquake. We never had the slightest idea that he would be with you. I can't believe that you didn't die in the raft, five days without food and water could have easily killed you. I know without a doubt God was with you every minute. Maybe this whole thing was for Nicholas sake. When you told me about the prayers you prayed that God would let him live so he could be saved. Knowing that if you died you would go the heaven, it just made me cry. I love you so much Liana."

"I love you to dad," she said kissing him on the cheek.

Liana's dad was a very distinguished looking person and when he was in the room people acknowledged him with respect. Just like the reporters had. Liana could tell that Nicholas liked him right away.

Liana worked hard that day, mostly to keep from thinking about Nicholas and every day after that.

On the third day Nicholas called her. When she heard his voice her heart skipped a beat.

"Liana how are you?"

"I'm great now that I'm talking to you," she said happily.

"Me to," he agreed.

"Hey, I've found some scripts that I think might be good movies, care if I come out tomorrow?"

"That would be great, do you know where we live?"

"Yeah, your dad gave me directions, Liana have you read any of the things the media are saying about you? Or heard what they're saying on the news?"

"No, how could I we don't get newspapers except the Farm Journal and of course, no TV."

"I'm going to bring some papers and magazines with me, I don't know what you all said to them, but they are treating you like little Virgin Mary!" He said excitedly.

"What?"

"Well, they seem to know all about your life and they love you. You'll have to explain this to me when I get there, the media never treats anybody this good, did your dad threaten them?"

"No, silly," she laughed, "After you called and told us about how they might take things the wrong way, my mom said that we all needed to talk to them and let them know just what kind of person Liana is. My dad agreed and when we got to the gate, the media were waiting. My dad got out of the car and talked to them, he invited them to the house. He gave them the run of the ranch while I took a wonderful bath.'

"I know what you mean, it felt fantastic to take a shower and shave. Then what happened?"

"Well, after my bath, I came downstairs and they were all seated in the living room having ice tea and coffee, leave it to my mom! Dad had already told them about our family and made it clear that we were Christians and that I had been raised with God's word."

"I set down with them and told them the whole story, from the earthquake, to the raft, to the island. I told them how we survived and about us both getting sick and how that led to your getting saved."

"Did you tell them about me kissing you and you shoving me down?"

Liana laughed, "No, silly."

"Oh, how I have missed your laugh. I miss you Liana, we were together for so long and my life isn't right without you being here. At night I go to bed and think about the cave and just knowing you were there, it's like part of me is missing."

"I know, sometimes I wish we were back on the island, I miss it."

5

THE NEXT DAY, Nicholas arrived about an hour before lunch. Liana ran out the door when she saw his car coming up the drive way. The drive way circled around the front of the house, he pulled up to the front porch. He got out and Liana ran to him and hugged him. They were both smiling, they both stepped back and looked at each other. Liana had put a very nice dress on, it was blue and was ankle length. Her hair was hanging long and straight and beautiful.

"You look sensational," he said looking at her all the way down, "and shoes, I've never seen you in shoes!"

"You look mighty nice yourself hombre," she said in a western swagger, "I can actually see your face, you can't be the same guy that I was on the island with, he was unshaven and looked more like a wild man."

They laughed, she grabbed his hand and pulled him into the house.

"Look ever body what the dogs dragged in."

Liana's family all greeted him happily, they sat and talked for some time than her mother invited them all into the kitchen to have lunch. They had a dining room, but always had lunch and breakfast at the kitchen table. The kitchen was a very big room and they had a table that seated twelve. Liana's mother had made a roast with potatoes and carrots, rolls and green beans.

"What a marvelous dinner, do you always have such an extraordinary lunch?" He asked.

"No," Alex said, "Only when we have company, this is why I was glad you were coming," he said jokingly.

"Well, this certainly makes me glad I came," Nicholas joked back.

They all sit down and enjoyed the lunch together, talking and laughing and eating hardily.

"I don't know about you Liana, but I just can't seem to get my fill of good food."

"I know what you mean, I lost twenty pounds on the island but, I am gaining it back pretty fast with mother's cooking. I hope I don't gain too much."

"Now, Liana," her mother said, "you have always been to thin, a little weight won't hurt you at all."

When they finished eating, Liana and Nicholas went to the family room, the others went back to work or home-schooling. Nicholas got his briefcase that he had carried in earlier and took the movie scripts out. He handed one to Liana and asked her to read it out loud.

It was a movie based on Christian values, but they decided it was too worldly for what they wanted, the second one, however, was very good, you could tell it was written by a true Christian.

"This one is great, I love it," she said.

"Then this is it, I thought it was the best to. Actually we need a story like what just happened to us," Nicholas said.

Then he looked at her and said, "That's exactly what we need, listen I can get a writer and you and I can tell our story to him. Then he can write a movie based on it, of course, it would have to be exactly how it happened and not a lot of made up stuff. What do you think?"

She looked at him with amazement, "You mean make a movie of our experience?"

"Sure, why not? True stories make a lot better movies than fiction, all the movies I've seen that are based on a true story are always better. Hey, maybe you and I could act in it together and tell it how it really happened. I think that would be a great movie and truly show how God worked, it would be incredible."

"I don't know how to act."

"It's easy, especially if you're remaking the exact thing that happened to you, all you have to do is be you."

"I don't know," she said hesitantly.

"Well, why don't you ask your family what they think? Maybe when I finish this movie we could do our story.

"Okay, I will at dinner tonight, you will stay for dinner won't you? I do want to show you around the ranch and I thought we might go horseback riding today."

"Sounds great, let's go look at the horses."

"Oh, by the way that reminds me, I don't know if you ever heard about the Weathersby's?"

"No, why."

"Well, they disappeared during the earthquake and have never been found."

"So, they were the other couple I heard about, that's very sad. I really liked them, they were wonderful people. I will miss them," he answered solemnly.

At the stable, they picked a horse out for Nicholas and Liana got hers. They rode for about thirty minutes when they came upon a small stream. Getting off the horses they lead them to the water. Then they set down on some rocks.

"This is the first time I've been out here, it's very beautiful and I think this place is nicer than the other ranch. I haven't seen it all yet, but there is more acreage here."

Nicholas was looking off in the distance when he said, "What's that," then he got on his horse and headed in the direction he had been looking.

Liana started riding after him, he had his horse running full speed. She could see a man by the fence ahead. When she came up behind Nicholas, she could hear them talking. It seems the guy was a reporter and had been taking pictures of them.

"What are you going to do with those pictures," Nicholas asked.

"What I always do with them, sell them to the highest bidder, of course, it's a free country."

"Well, kid, looks like you got the pictures you wanted, now give me your name and phone number, in case I have a story to tell you. You seem like a real go getter."

The guy said he would be glad to and gave Nicolas his card with his name and number on it.

"Now," Nicolas said dramatically, "Let me tell you what is going to happen to you if anything bad about Ms. Baugh is written with these pictures. Ms. Baugh is a devout Christian and she is nothing like you and me. Because I'm rich and will be able to do it, I will make you lose everything you have ever had if you sell these to a sleazy tabloid and they say terrible things about her. Do you get my meaning?"

"Yeah, sure, I've read what the media are saying about her and I wouldn't want to be the one to say anything differently."

"Now, if I see something good come out of these pictures, I will reward you nicely."

Nicholas handed him his card and told him this was his agent's number and if he felt like he needed a reward to just call his agent and tell him what happened here. The guy agreed and took Nicholas' card and left.

"So, you have to bribe them to say good things?" She questioned.

He grinned and said, "Sometimes it is best. When we get back I don't want to forget to show you and your family what the media is saying about you, it's astonishing."

When they got back, he got the magazines and newspapers out and showed them to the Baugh's.

"Oh," Bella said, "These articles are wonderful, if dad hadn't invited them in and talked to them it probably wouldn't have happened this way."

"That was extraordinary, what a good idea and that is why they are talking about Liana the way they are. Who would ever have thought to talk to them like that? Usually people want to be left alone and I'm sure you did, but instead you told them all about her so they wouldn't make up a bunch of stuff. That was the best thing you could have done, it worked to, I mean look at these articles they make Liana very special, as they should. You should hear what they are saying on TV, according to them, of course, I'm a rake and they sympathized with poor Liana for having to stay on the island with me! The media really likes you, Liana and I am very thankful."

"Me to," her dad said, then he told Nicholas that it was Liana's mother who said we needed to talk to them and tell them about Liana so they wouldn't make up a lot of nonsense about her.

Nicholas patted Emily on the back and said, "Good job."

When Nicholas left, Liana walked him out to the car. He took her hands in his and told her he had a really great day.

"Will you come back soon?" she asked, "I know you must be very busy with your friends."

He could tell she was questioning his past women, "Liana you mustn't worry about my friends. I am a changed man and I haven't any friends except you and your family and the new people I have met in the church I started going to. When I have tried to talk to my friends about God, they aren't interested and they say they miss the old me. I tell them the old me is gone that I am a new man in Christ and I hardly ever hear from any of them."

Then he said, "I'll be back as soon as I can and I'll keep in touch with you about the movie."

"Okay."

He let go of her hands and pulled her to him and gave her a hug, kissing her on the forehead. While he was holding her, he whispered that he bought a bible.

"You did," she asked?

"Yes, and in my spare time I have been reading it and because of you, I actually understand what I'm reading," he said smiling at her. "Actually, I'm not in a real big hurry to make a movie, I would like to study the bible first, that way, maybe I can make the movie right. I am going to church Sunday and talking to the preacher to maybe get somebody to help me with a study and I know I need to get baptized soon. When I do will you come? I wish we lived closer to each other so we could go the church together."

She was so happy, "I wish we did to, of course, I'll come to your baptism, I hope it is soon, because I will be leaving for Venezuela in a month."

He sounded disappointed, "Are you still going to work in the mission."

"Yes, but it will be a while."

"Liana I have so much to learn and my desire is to live a good Godly life, it's a whole new world for me and I like it. I've always been so busy with parties and worldly stuff and this new way of living is totally challenging to me. I love it, I just hope I can do it right."

"God knows your heart Nicholas and he will be with you all the way, he always blesses the ones he loves and I know he will bless you for doing this."

Nicholas left and they both were lonely immediately, not being able to tell each other how they really felt was so hard.

A few days passed before Nicholas called her again. He wanted to call her every day, but was afraid she would get tired of it. The day she shoved him away was still fresh in his mind and he was being cautious about letting her know how he felt. Maybe, he shouldn't be so careful, sometimes he thought she really liked him more than just a friend. But, he couldn't take the chance.

When he called, he told her all about his bible study and they had an incredible conversation. They were able to talk equally about the bible, he was a fast study and all the time on the island with her telling him all the stories he was able learn God's word and understand it.

"By the way, I'm getting baptized next Sunday, can you come?"

"Of course, my whole family wants to come to it if that's okay with you."

"That would be great, I'll take you all to my favorite place for dinner after words."

"Sounds wonderful, I can't wait to see you again."

"Me to, let me give you directions to the church."

He gave her directions and told her what time to be there then they told each other good night.

She lay in bed so excited she couldn't sleep she thought about all the things that God and done to bring Nicholas to where he was. It was so unbelievable and she was so glad God had let her be a part of it.

Sunday came and the family was up early, it was a long way to Hollywood. They had never been there and were excited about seeing it. In Hollywood, they pulled up to a huge church, it was beautiful. As they walked up to the front steps Nicholas was standing there waiting for them. He met them with a smile and took Liana's arm as they walked in. There were a few reporters there, only the ones he invited, they were being very discrete. Nicholas had told

Liana that he wanted this most important time in his life to be recorded. And if they showed it to the world that was even better.

In the baptismal pool the pastor baptized him in the name of the Father, Son and Holy Spirit. Liana knew all the angels in heaven were singing.

From the church they rode with Nicholas in a limousine to the restaurant. The limo parked in front of a huge building downtown, they rode the elevator to the top floor and walked into a magnificent restaurant. It was in a circular shape and had glass windows from floor to ceiling all around it. There was an orchestra playing some lovely music. The host led them to a table by the window overlooking the city.

After they were seated, Alex said, "So this is Hollywood, funny I thought it would be a lot fancier."

They all laughed. The waiter brought goblets of water.

And Alex continued with his antics, "I would like to make a toast," they all picked up their glasses and Alex said "To Nicholas, our brother in Christ, may your life with God be more exciting than anything that has ever happened to you before!"

They all agreed and tipped their glasses to each other's. They had an extraordinary dinner and then Nicholas asked them to come to his house for a while. On the way they drove through Hollywood and Nicholas pointed out all the attractions. He also told the stories of how all the rich people tried to outdo each other by buying some of the most ridiculous stuff. He had them laughing throughout the drive. When they pulled into his driveway there was a beautiful rock wall about ten feet tall surrounding the place. The driver pulled up to a phone and after he said something the entry gate opened.

The drive was circular and was made of big flat rocks like the fence, at the door the limo driver got out and opened their door for them. Alex and Bella were loving it.

"Wow!" Bella said, "Look at this house!"

"I think I could stand to live here," Alex said smiling.

The door was opened by a woman, Nicholas introduced her as the head housekeeper Jessie. She nodded acknowledgement to them and left.

"How many rooms does this mansion have," Bella asked?

"About a dozen or so," Nicholas answered.

He led them into a big room with a pool table and some game tables, three overstuffed sofas and a huge fireplace.

"This is the room where I entertain mostly, I bought a very special game to play tonight," he told them.

He took a box off a table and showed it to them, it was Bible Trivia.

"Anybody care to play? But, I must warn you I have cheated, I've been using this to help me study," he said with a smile.

"I'll give it a go," Dan said.

The rest of them chimed in and agreed that it would be fun. They all set at the table and Nicholas told them the rules. They decided to play men against women since they had equal numbers. They were all having a great time, laughing when someone missed and yelling when they made points. Jessie brought iced tea for them and some snacks, she smiled when she saw how much fun they were having.

"Who's winning," she asked.

"We are," Alex said excitedly.

"No you're not, we're ahead of you," Bella said.

They all laughed and when the game was over Bella asked if they could see the house. He was happy to show them. The entire place was beautiful and it had an inside and outside pool. Nicholas told them next time they came to bring their suits. They agreed that would be great.

They went outside to the grounds and walked around in a breathtaking garden. Liana was in awe and told him so.

"You really are rich," she said, "You've really been blessed."

"Yes, and since I have gotten saved, I look at all this stuff in a totally different way. Before it was important to have everything, but now I see it as only stuff and can think of so much more important things I can do with my money."

"Well, you know Jesus said to help the widows and the children. There's so many that need help."

"Yes, and I've been giving that a lot of thought," he told her.

"That's wonderful Nicholas."

Dan and Emily came up and told them they had a long drive home and maybe they should get going.

Nicholas rode with them back to the church where their car was parked. They all got out and said their goodbyes except Liana. Liana wanted a moment alone with him to tell him she was leaving for Venezuela in two weeks and hoped she would see him before she left.

"Must you go? I can't imagine you being that far away," he asked.

"My Aunt Kim and Uncle Mike really need help, they have been talking to us a lot lately and there are so many children living on the streets there that they can't begin to help all of them. They really need my help to teach and take care of the little ones."

"I will come see you before you leave, do you think your parents would allow me to take you out?"

Liana wasn't thinking and before she could stop herself she said, "You mean on a date?"

"Well, I guess it would be or it could be just two friends spending time together."

"Oh, yeah, well I think they would let me go, they really like you and since I will be gone so long they'll understand that we want to spend some time together."

"I'll call your dad to get permission, isn't that how it's done?"

She smiled, "If you call my dad and ask permission that means it is a date."

"Okay, it's a date, will you go out with me?"

When she said yes, his heart skipped a beat, they were actually going on a date.

He kissed her on the cheek and said, "You better go on, they're waiting for you."

She got out of the car and before she got into her parents car, she turned and blew him a kiss. He laughed, he was so excited and he smiled all the way home. He knew that in Liana's family that they only dated someone if they thought they might marry them someday. He could tell Liana wanted it to be a date, 'maybe he has a chance after all,' he thought.

6

NICHOLAS WAS TRUE to his word and the very next day he called Dan and asked if he could take Liana out. Dan told him that it would be fine, he said he knew that Nicholas had always been a gentleman towards Liana and knew he would continue to be.

Their date started at ten in the morning, he had a surprise for her and wanted her to wear only comfortable shorts and to bring a swimming suit. He had already talked to her dad and he agreed to let him land a helicopter in their field.

Liana didn't know about the helicopter and when he landed she couldn't believe it. He got her on the helicopter and told her they were going to visit their island. Liana was so excited she threw her arms around him and hugged him.

"I can't believe it!" She said with great excitement, "how did you think of that?"

"Well, it is the place where I was the happiest I have ever been and I thought you might like to go back."

"Oh yes, I can't wait to see it, can you imagine all we went through and ended up on that island and had to survive, we really should hate that island, but instead we actually love it."

"Putting it that way it is kind of weird," he laughed.

The helicopter circled the island and they could see it very well when they flew over the waterfall, it looked so beautiful. The copter landed not far from the pool. The pilot got out and started carrying a big basket over by the pool of water. He spread a blanket and set the basket on it. Nicholas took his bag and liana's bag and talked to the pilot. Then the pilot got into the copter and flew away.

Nicholas looked at her and said, "Don't worry, he's coming back."

She smiled and said, "I'm not worried, even if he didn't come back we would be okay, we know how to survive here."

"Want to go for a swim before we eat?"

"Yeah, that would be nice," she said, "I'll go to the cave and change."

He had worn his swimsuit and had dry clothes in his bag. When Liana came out of the cave, he had to catch his breath. She was beautiful, she had on a modest two piece, most of the women he knew wore thongs and he thought Liana looked much better.

They went into the pool and swam around, talking and laughing, they talked about the time he ducked her, but she refused to give in so he ducked her again.

"You were very stubborn, you would have drowned before you gave in!"

When they got out they dried off and had lunch, Jessie had fixed it and it was delicious. After eating they lay back on the blanket and talked some more.

"I know you told your aunt and uncle you'd come to Venezuela and I know they need you, but I'm a little worried about you going there. That country is not safe for beautiful girls like you Liana. I've read that a lot of women are kidnapped there and sold as slaves. I'm really going to worry about you."

"The mission that my aunt and uncle have is fully enclosed by high walls, I've seen pictures. My aunt said there is a police station a block away, she said if she thought it was dangerous for me that they wouldn't have me come. I'm not too worried about it."

"Let's go for a walk and look at our island," he suggested.

"That sounds great."

They walked over most of the island and when they returned, the helicopter was there waiting for them. They had put on dry clothes before they went for the walk and the pilot had already stored all their things in the copter.

It was just turning dusk when they took off, "bye, bye little island," Liana said as they flew away.

At home that night, Liana thought about the day. It had been wonderful she wished she could spend every day with him. She had hoped he might have kissed her, if he had asked, she would have said yes. But, he was a perfect gentlemen and treated her with great respect.

The day had come for her to leave for Venezuela, Nicholas had asked if he could take her to the airport. So Liana said her good-byes to her family and rode with him to the airport. They arrived early and while they were setting in the waiting area Nicholas told her he knew he would miss her too much and would inevitably be flying out to see her. This made her very happy.

When they called her flight she stood up to go, but Nicholas took hold of her arm and turned her to him, "May I kiss you," he asked.

"Yes," she said without hesitation.

He pulled her to him and kissed her tenderly, she didn't push him away this time and she put her arms around his neck and kissed back.

"You're not blushing," he smiled.

"I'm going to miss you so much," she said sadly.

They called her flight again and she turned and walked toward the plane, he stood there watching her, she turned and smiled and threw him a kiss, he threw her one back and she walked away.

When the plane landed, her aunt and uncle were waiting for her. They hugged her and took her bags to the car. After leaving the airport they drove through the big city of Caracas. Aunt Kim and Uncle Mike pointed out many interesting things on the way. They asked about her family, Aunt Kim was Liana's mother's sister. She wanted to know everything that was going on. She said Emily had told her all about the earthquake and all that had happened to Liana. They talked and enjoyed the ride.

Where they finally stopped was on the west side of the city. Uncle Mike pulled up to some big wooden doors and honked the horn, a short time later the doors were opened by a young man. Uncle Mike drove into a big inner court. He parked the car and they got out. Children of all ages came running up to them. Kim introduced them to Liana and told them she was their new teacher. They smiled and told her hi and one of them gave her a hug.

"Come on Liana," Uncle Mike said, "Let's get you settled into your room and then we'll have some dinner."

The courtyard was huge and the two story building surrounded it so the courtyard was totally enclosed. There was a walk-way all around the building on second floor. Inside the place was very old, but clean. They took Liana to a room on second floor that looked out over the courtyard. It was a small room with a bed and dresser, the dresser had a mirror on it and there was a small desk in the corner.

"I know, this is not what you are used to Liana, but we are pretty poor here. We're lucky to get enough money each month to buy food and clothing for the children."

"This is fine Aunt Kim, I understand and I hope I won't become a burden to you. All you have to do is show me what you want and I'll do it."

"We know you will," Uncle Mike agreed, "We know all of Dan's children have good work ethics." He smiled.

Then Kim told her to get comfortable and dinner will be ready soon, they would call her when it was ready. Liana told them thanks and decided to unpack. The closet was small, but big enough for her clothes. She put her garments in the dresser and put her toiletries on top of it. She had brought a few books and some writing paper, she set them neatly on the desk.

When she finished Liana stepped out on the walk-way that overlooked the courtyard. The children were playing, some had an old basketball and there was a basketball basket in one area of the courtyard where they were playing basketball. Others were playing in different areas. She saw some little girls with dolls and could tell they were playing house.

The dinner tablet was one of the biggest she had ever seen, it was in a large room and the children were already seated when she came in. The plates had already been filled with food and was setting on the table. Aunt Kim patted a chair next to hers and Liana set down. When Uncle Mike came in they all rose from their seats and he gave the grace.

The food was very good, Liana told her aunt that, and Kim said, "Thank you, I'm glad you like it, I have trained some of the girls to cook."

"Well, you did a good job than because it is delicious."

Kim introduced her to the girls who cooked, they were setting across the table. They all smiled and greeted each other. They were probably fifteen or sixteen.

"I noticed you have children here of all ages," Liana said.

"Yes, it doesn't matter what age they are, they all need help. If any are old enough, we get them jobs so they can help pay the bills. The problem is there's not many jobs for young people, that's why they live here."

That night after the children were all in their beds, Kim and Mike told Liana the stories about the children. Kim and Mike had come here to start a church ministry, but when they saw all the homeless children, their hearts were broken and they decided to do all they could for the children instead.

"How many children do you have here?"

"Right now, we have fifty-five, sometimes we have more. Most of the children we get are off the streets, but sometimes the young girls who have babies just bring them here and leave them. Most of the children are ten and up, the babies get adopted usually. We have found them as young as two living on the streets." Mike informed her.

"You're kidding!"

"No, one day we found three children on the street a two year old, a four year old and a ten year old, the ten year old was their sister and she was trying to take care of them."

"Oh, no, that makes me want to cry," Liana said.

"It did make us cry," Kim said with sadness in her voice.

That night Liana thought about all the terrible stories her aunt and uncle had told her. She was so glad she came and was ready to help in any way possible.

Liana got into the swing of things pretty fast, she thought she would be teaching classes, but a school bus actually picked up the children on week days. What Liana did was help any of the children who needed help with homework and she helped the ones that was way behind because they hadn't been going to school. Kim told her this really had taken a big burden off them. On the days when the children were in school, Liana cleaned most of the time and helped cook whenever she could. The teenage girls loved Liana and had lots of fun with her when she helped them cook. And now that Liana was here, Kim had more time to take care of more pressing things.

Every Sunday they had church, one of the teenage boys had a beautiful voice and always led the singing. Liana loved listening to them sing, it brought joy to her heart. Mike was very good with them and they really liked him, he was able to teach about the bible in a way they could understand it.

Liana's Spanish was really being tested. She studied Spanish for three years, but still found it a little difficult to communicate. She had a lot of fun with the kids when they had to do charades to get her to understand. But, on the most part she was able to communicate pretty well.

Liana had been there nearly a month now. Nicholas called her weekly and kept her up-to-date on his movie. They missed each other terribly and it was evident when they talked. Luckily they were both so busy they didn't have time to dwell on it.

One day he told her, "I don't think I can wait till the movie is done before I come out there, I may have to put it on hold. I'm afraid you will meet someone and fall in love with him, before we even have our second date."

She laughed, "You don't have to worry about that, believe me there is nothing glamorous about this job and I never leave the place unless Aunt Kim needs me to help when she buys groceries. Oh, Nicholas I have never seen such poverty. We manage to feed the children and cloth them, but are not able to get anything except the bare essentials. The government won't help at all and the money we get is from donations. And, I know most of the people who donate don't have much either. If you were out here it would break your heart."

"It's that bad?" He questioned. "I had no idea Liana, listen I don't want you to worry your pretty head about that any more, I am going to give you guys some help. Remember when we talked about how God had blessed me? Well, I know now that all of this isn't even mine. It all belongs to God and I intend to do the right thing with it. I have been busy with the movie and have been trying so hard to get it done so I can come to see you that I never got around to helping anyone. Now, I can do that."

"My Aunt and Uncle will be so pleased Nicholas. We can use all the help we can get."

"Well, it's coming, when I get off the phone with you, I'll set it in motion."

The next day Kim got a phone call from a prominent bank in Caracas they asked her to come in and talk to them.

"I really can't," she said, "If you need to talk to me, you'll have to come out here."

The banker was surprised, but agreed to come there and talk to them. Kim had no idea what he wanted and Liana hadn't had the chance to tell her about Nicholas and her phone call last night.

He was there about an hour later, Kim invited him in and offered him tea. He told her that would be nice and waited on the sofa for her to come with it. She sat the tea cup down and offered sugar and milk, he said he liked his black and took a drink. He complimented her on how good it was and then she asked him why he was there.

"Well," he said, "You and your husband have been given a very large amount of money, it was wired to our bank this morning."

"What," she asked?

"Do you know a man named Nicholas Reeves, I believe he is a famous actor in the U. S."

"Yes, he is a friend of my niece who is staying with us and helping us."

"Well, he wired you a half a million dollars."

"What?"

"Yes, we opened you an account in our bank and I have brought the papers for you and your husband to sign for the checking account."

She was astounded and told him she would go find her husband.

She found Mike changing the oil in their car, "I don't know how much longer this car is going to hold up," he stopped talking when he saw her face, "What's wrong?" He asked.

She explained to him what just happened and he couldn't believe it.

"It's true," she said, "Come on in now and don't keep this man waiting.

Mike walked in and the banker stood up, he introduced himself and then they shook hands.

After they had signed the papers and the banker left, they couldn't hold it in any longer. They grabbed each other and started yelling and laughing. Liana heard the commotion and ran in to see what was wrong.

"What's wrong?"

"Nothing is wrong, everything is right," Mike said.

After they told Liana what happened, she grabbed them and started jumping up and down yelling and laughing to. Then Aunt Kim set down and put her face in her hands and started crying, Liana and Mike set on each side of her and hugged her.

"I really didn't think I could go on much longer the way we've been living. I know that sounds selfish, but the children needed so much more then we could give them. And we were always worried where the next money would come from." She said still crying.

Mike handed her some tissues and said, "I know my dear, I was feeling the same way, when Liana came to help that made things a little easier, but it was still too hard."

Liana kissed her Aunt Kim and said, "You guys have given up so much to be here to help the children, God is no doubt blessing you for that now."

Kim smiled through her tears and took Liana's hand, "Thank you Liana for coming, you don't know how much that means to us. And we must thank Nicholas, the next time he calls, tell him how much we thank him for what he has done."

"I will, Aunt Kim, now you need to figure out what you are going to do with that money."

"That won't be hard," she said, "They need everything."

That night Nicholas called, Liana was so excited, "Oh, Nicholas that was the most wonderful thing you did. You'll never know how much you have helped these children. Aunt Kim and Uncle Mike are ecstatic, they were at their wits end when this happened, Aunt Kim has been crying all day."

"Why is she crying, from happiness I hope?"

"Yes silly, from happiness."

She continued, "But Nicholas are you sure you can afford to do that, that's a lot of money and I would really feel bad if you couldn't afford it."

"Don't worry, Liana, I'll be fine, by the way, we are taking a break on the movie for a couple of weeks, so I am coming out as soon as I can get a ticket."

"No way!"

"Yes, way, I'll be there in three days."

Liana's heart was beating fast, "I can't wait that long."

He laughed, "Me either, but it will come sooner than you think."

When they hung up, Liana ran to tell her aunt and uncle. They were all in a tizzy for the three days waiting on Nicholas. The day of his arrival, Liana put on her prettiest dress and her hair was shining, she looked beautiful. Her aunt and uncle said she had never been prettier.

They met him at the airport in the old station wagon, When Liana saw him walk into the airport, he took her breath away, he was so handsome. His eyes lit up when he saw her and they hurried to each other and hugged.

He held her out from him and looked at her, "You're even more beautiful than the last time I saw you."

"So are you," she laughed.

"Oh, you think I'm beautiful? I thought men were handsome."

"You're beautiful though," she said teasingly.

She grabbed his hand and took him to meet Kim and Mike. They shook hands and Kim started right in thanking him for helping them with the children. He told her he was more than happy to and he hoped it would make a difference. Kim assured him it would.

"Are you hungry," Mike asked?

"Yes, I think I could use something to eat."

"Good," Mike said, "I was hoping you would be, so we could eat at my favorite restaurant. Have you ever been here before?"

"No, this is my first trip to Venezuela."

"The local cuisine is very good if you like Spanish food."

"Love it."

"Good, let's go have some of the best salsa ever."

They laughed and as they drove Mike told Nicholas some of the history of Caracas. Their meal was excellent.

"That dinner was incredible." Nicholas told them.

"I haven't ever been disappointed there," Mike answered.

As they pulled into the orphanage Nicholas noticed how ran down it was and when they pulled into the courtyard, Mike said, "You can see how badly we needed the help you have given us. This place looks really bad, but it really is nicer than anything any of the children have ever lived in. It looks like a mansion next to the slums in this town."

The children playing outside smiled and waved at them, "You know no matter how bad they have it, they still smile, they just break my heart," Kim said.

"I know what you mean," Liana agreed.

When they got out of the car, Nicholas went over to the children and asked each their name and shook their hand. He picked up one little girl and gave her a kiss. The children loved him!

Liana showed Nicholas to his room, it was next to hers and was as bare as hers was. They took his stuff in and she apologized for the room.

"Liana, don't apologize for this room to me, what you and your aunt and uncle are doing is the most wonderful thing I have ever seen. I regret that I haven't been involved in helping people before this. I've been wasting my money on ridiculous extravagant things when I could have been doing a lot of good with it."

"I adore you," she said earnestly.

He smiled, he wanted so badly to tell her he loved her, but he managed to hold back.

"I adore you to, you are an amazing person to be so young, I can't imagine what you will be like when you're seventy, probably the smartest person in the world."

She laughed, "Probably."

Now he laughed, "Come on let's go talk with Mike and Kim and maybe we can make some plans on what we are going to do with this place."

"Are you going to help us?"

"I would love to, if you guys will let me."

"That would be fantastic," they walked into the living room where Kim and Mike were, "Guess what!" Liana said.

"What?" Kim asked.

"Nicholas wants to help us with this place."

"That's wonderful."

"Yes, I would like to maybe find a bigger place for you, it looks like you're getting overcrowded. Maybe tomorrow Liana and I can go looking, that is if you can spare her."

"Of course, we can, she needs a break from here anyway. The only place she's gone since she's been here is the grocery store with me and believe me that is no fun."

They talked for a couple of hours, Nicholas asked them what sort of things they might need that might be helpful.

Mike said, "You know we talk to the government all the time asking them to start some kind of program to help these kids, but they don't seem to care."

"So, it's just left to people like you to step in and take care of them."

"That's right, there's really nobody who seems to care what happens to these kids, from what I've learned, it's been this way forever." Mike told him.

They talked until it was time for the women to put the children to bed. The older girls always made sure the younger ones had their baths and helped them get ready. Liana started to go with Kim, but Kim told her she could take care of it tonight so Liana stayed with Nicholas.

Mike excused himself, he said he had to get up at the crack of dawn tomorrow, they all said good night and Nicolas and Liana was left alone.

7

"WHAT DO YOU do around here in your spare time," Nicholas asked.

"We have very little spare time, usually after all the kids are in bed, I'm so tired I get my bath and go to bed. It's just one day running into another here. Sometimes I read, but not often."

"Well, it looks like they gave you a day off tomorrow so we will make the most of it."

"Sounds sensational."

They went out in the courtyard, it was pretty dark because there was only one light by the back door.

"What's the movie like," she asked?

"I think you will really like it. It's gone exceptionally well, it should finish ahead of schedule."

He sat down on a bench and pulled her down beside him, he put his arm around her and held her close to him, "This is better," he said, "If we were on our Island, we could have a campfire."

She lay against his shoulder and said, "That would be nice, but it wouldn't matter where we were, as long as we were setting together like this I would be happy."

He looked down at her, "Would you?"

"Yes, you know I love to be with you."

For a minute he thought she was going to say she loved him, but he would take, love to be with you, "and I love to be with you to."

That was the closest they had come to saying they loved each other. And both were very aware of it.

Before he even knew what he was doing, he had turned her head and kissed her, it was more passionate then their last kiss. She didn't resist, but when it was over she stood up and grabbed his hand and ran towards to house.

"Are you leaving me?" He asked.

"Yes," she said smiling, "You have to quit fooling around sir or you will surely win my heart and then you will leave me sad."

"I will never leave you dear lady, I hold you in the highest esteem and will never make you sad."

She hugged him and kissed him on the cheek and ran to her bedroom.

He smiled and thought that was the cutest way he had ever seen for someone to get out of a situation that they didn't know how to handle.

All she could think about was the kiss, she had never felt that way before, she loved it, but it frightened her at the same time. She knew she was very much in love with him, but she didn't know if he loved her or just really liked her. How could he be in love with her when he could have any woman it the world, she didn't even compare to the beautiful women he knew.

He on the other hand felt like she might love him, but maybe she was afraid he wasn't serious and that he might leave her.

Next morning she put on a lovely sun dress and sandals, she knew they were going to look at other places for the orphanage. When she walked into the living room, he was already up and waiting for her. He stood up and told her how pretty she looked when she came in.

"You look pretty to sir."

"Thank you," he smiled knowing she was teasing him from the last time she called him beautiful.

He had hired a car, when they went out it was waiting for them.

"This is wonderful," she said, "I really needed this, I was getting stir crazy being in the orphanage all the time."

"I'm glad I came to rescue you, if you want we can go have breakfast first and then I have arranged to have a real estate agent show us some possible properties that might work better for the orphanage."

"You have been a busy man that all sounds great, I love just setting back and letting you make the plans."

He took her to a very nice restaurant and the breakfast was very wholesome and delicious. Than they met with the agent. Every property that they looked at was magnificent, he asked her opinion of each one. The one they both liked was a lovely Spanish Villa. It was as big as a castle with an enormous veranda, it set on top of a hill and looked down over the city. There was a massive gate at the bottom of the hill and the driveway went all the way up the hill.

A large water fountain was in front, the rooms were perfect most of them were large and would accommodate three or four beds, the dining hall was vast, they could put several tables in it, enough for all of the children to eat at once. In the back was an even bigger veranda then the front with a very nice swimming pool.

"This is enormous, this would probably house a hundred children." She told him.

"Do you think the kids would be happy here?" He said smiling.

"Are you kidding, anybody would be happy here," she said laughing.

"Well, I say we show it to Kim and Mike and see what they think."

"This has got to cost a small fortune, are you serious?"

"You let me worry about the cost, there's nothing too good for these children."

The next morning, they took Kim and Mike to see the villa. When they saw it, they were both worried about the cost.

"You mustn't worry about that, just tell me if this would work. If you want it, not only will I get it for you, but I will make sure all utilities are paid. I know you wouldn't have enough probably to pay for utilities in this big a place and

I want you to be able to take care of the children without worrying about things like that. As a matter of fact, I am making out a trust to make sure this place is taken care of long after I'm dead. Before I became a Christian, I never even thought about things like this, the poor and starving. I didn't even know homeless children existed, well, maybe I knew, but I never thought about it. Now, when I see people like you, giving up everything to help somebody, I am ashamed of myself. I have a lot of making up to do and I am going to start with these children. There's no reason they can't live in a place like this, after what they have been through, they deserve it a lot more than most people."

"This place will be so perfect," Kim said, "and God will bless you greatly."

"Don't you see Aunt Kim and Uncle Mike, this is a great blessing from God for you, for all you have done. You have given up everything to help these children and God is blessing you through Nicholas."

"Yes," Nicholas said, don't rob me of my blessing of being able to give this to you."

At that, they all laughed and became light hearted.

"Oh, my, gosh," Kim said, "I can't believe we are really going to live here and bring the children here, this is one of the best days of my life."

"It's settled then I'll tell them we will take it, now how about going to lunch for a little celebration."

"We can do that," Mike said, "Then Kim and I will have to get back to the orphanage."

"Yeah, I better go back with you," Liana said, "I know what it's like there when we are shorthanded."

"Then I will go and seal the deal with the realtors."

They had lunch at a small outdoor café then Liana went with Kim and Mike back to the orphanage.

When they got to the orphanage, they found a new child there with only one eye, the other eye had been sewn shut. One of the teenage girls told them he just showed up and asked if anybody could help him find his parents. The boy said his name was Justin Delgado and he was twelve years old. He told them a man had taken him out of his yard and then they took his eye out and cut his back and that he had escaped from them and was looking for his family.

Mike said, "Would you please let me see your back."

The boy didn't hesitate he turned and pulled his shirt up and there on the right side by his waist was a perfect straight line scar.

Mike wanted to cry, but he kept his composure, he told the girl to take the boy inside and find him something very good to eat. The boy could speak English and he smiled and went with the girl.

Mike looked at Kim and Liana and said, "This child has had his organs harvested, I have heard about stuff like this, but have never been faced with it."

Liana and Kim both put their hand over their mouths in astonishment, "Oh, no," Kim said and began crying, Liana cried to, "Oh that poor child."

Mike put his arms around both women and held them while they cried, "We will have to call the police, but they may not do anything, I'm afraid that they will take the boy and hush it up."

"Please, would you not call them until Nicholas returns?" Liana asked.

"Yes, we will wait for him and see if he has any suggestions, in the meantime, I'm going to try to find his parents.

You girls go ahead and tend to the kids and get dinner and I'll try to find them. The way the boy talked, he was kidnapped from his own yard."

When Nicholas arrived, he had the title of the property in his hand, "You may move whenever you wish," he told the girls.

Then he saw the look on their faces and asked, "What's wrong?"

"Oh, Nicholas you won't believe what has happened." Liana answered.

He went to Liana and took her arms looking into her eyes, "What?"

Liana and Kim told him about the boy, he was applauded, about that time Mike came in and said, "I think I found his parents. I haven't talked to them yet, I wanted to wait till Nicholas got here and see what he thinks we should do."

Nicholas was furious, "How could anybody do such a despicable thing. We need to get the police and have them after the tyrants that did this."

Mike told Nicholas that he really didn't think the police would do anything, that some of the police here were nothing but thugs and are probably in on selling these organs. He said he really didn't trust any of them, the only thing they were interested in was if it would make them any money. He told him he was sure there were some good cops there, but he wouldn't know who to trust. He also told Nicholas that he thought the boy may be half white with a name like Justin because there were very few Spanish boys with American names.

Nicholas asked to have the boy brought in. When Nicholas saw his eye, he wanted to cry. He hugged the boy and told him that they were trying to find his parents. The boy said they lived on El Rio Street.

"That's the address I found on them, I think the first thing we should do is reunite him with his family," Mike suggested.

"Without a doubt we need to take him home, but I am not just going to take him home and let that be the end of it. Somebody is going to pay for this crime."

They decided that Nicholas and Mike would drive the boy home and talk to the parents. They put the boy in the front seat of the car with them and drove to his house. Upon arriving, a man came out of the house with a questioning look on his face. Nicholas got out and the boy climbed out and ran past him.

When his father saw his son, he fell on his knees and wept. The mother came out to see what was going on, she was blonde headed, possibly American. She saw Justin and started screaming, she ran to him and hugged him, and his father was hugging them both. She kissed him all over his face drying his tears. The reunion was too much for Nicholas and Mike to take, they also went over with tears in their eyes and patted the mother and father on the back.

Two children younger than Justin came out the door, Justin broke loose and ran to them. They were yelling his name and jumping up and down with glee.

"Where did you find him and what is wrong with his eye." his mother asked?

We didn't find him, he found us, I'm Mike Hamilton and this is Nicholas Reeves, I have an orphanage across town and the boy just showed up today. He said some men took him right out of the yard."

The father said he was Julio Delgado and his wife's name was Beth. He told them that three months ago his boy did disappear out of the yard and they had not seen him since. He started thanking Mike and Nicholas for bringing him home.

"It was a pleasure to bring him home," Nicholas spoke, "But Mr. Delgado, there is much more to this then him just coming home. Some criminals have taken one of his eyes and a kidney to sell in the black market."

Julio sucked in his breath, he was aghast, "Are you sure?"

"Yes, the boy told us these men did this to him. We haven't taken him to the doctor yet, because we know if a doctor examines the boy, the doctor will have to turn this into the law."

"Oh, no, we do not trust the police please do not tell them, they might take our boy from us."

"See what I mean," commented Mike. "The locals distrust the police as much as I do."

"Yes, we distrust the police," Beth said. "When this happened they didn't even try to find him. They blamed us and said he ran away, but we knew he didn't. And we have friends who have lost children and the police did not do a thing. We think the cops are doing it."

The more Nicholas heard the angrier he became, "This is outrageous, I have never heard anything like this before and to use children in this way. Trust me Mr. and Mrs. Delgado somebody will pay for this."

The Delgado's believed him and invited the men into their house. It was a small house but very clean.

After they set down Julio told them he had a friend that was a doctor they and would take the boy to him. He was sure the doctor would not say anything to the authorities.

"Are you American?" Mike asked Beth.

"Yes, I grew up in New Mexico and my parents came here to teach and I've been here ever since."

"Well, it is quite possible that the American Embassy may step into this, since you are from America."

"That is a very good possibility," Nicholas agreed. "Also I know how to stir up a lot of publicity." He grinned, then continued, "I think something would be done if this was to go internationally. I know the Americans would not stand for it and for that matter not many countries would. If this is made public for the world to see, I'm sure something would be done. This is probably one of the most horrific offenses I have ever heard of and those responsible must be stopped. They need to make an example of them with the death penalty and maybe that would stop others from doing it. I have some Governor friends that I could get involved and they could take it to a higher level." Nicholas added, then said, "All the media would jump on a story like this, I think we could stop this sort of thing worldwide if the penalties were great enough."

He looked at Julio and Beth and asked if they thought they could handle a lot of publicity on this matter. They said they would do whatever it took to stop this from happening. Nicholas warned them that they would be going crazy with reporters always at their door and sometimes the media doesn't say very nice things about people.

"That is okay," Beth stated. "We must do what has to be done to stop this."

"That's the spirit," Nicholas told her. "And you won't be alone, we will be right there with you."

That night Nicholas and Mike told the women everything that was said. Nicholas also told them something else.

"Now I have some good news. Remember this morning when I told you, that you could move whenever you want?"

With curiosity in her voice, Liana said, "Yes."

"Well, I have hired a moving company and they are going to move you next Wednesday. But, the only thing you need to pack is your clothing and personal belongings."

"What about the furniture?" Questioned Kim.

"I have a company who has already started furnishing the place. I told them how many beds and they will also furnish all the bedding and everything you need to keep house with, such as pots and pans and dishes and so on. So, unless there is some piece of furniture or utensils or anything like that, that you can't bear to leave behind, you may take it. Otherwise, if I haven't thought of everything, please bring it to my attention so we can get it for you."

Liana was thrilled, she ran and hugged him and showered him with kisses on his face.

He held her to him and looking down at her said, "Wow, if I had known I would get this kind of response, I would have done this much sooner." She laughed and stepped back.

Kim and Mike didn't miss the look in his eyes when he looked at her. The first day he came, Mike told her that Nicholas was in love with Liana and now, she saw it too.

Early Tuesday morning before Liana had gotten dressed, there was a knock on the door. She grabbed her robe and ran to the door. Several people were standing there, Liana recognized Jessie.

In a confused tone, Liana said, "Jessie what are you doing here?"

"Nicholas wanted to surprise you and bring us out here to help, we closed the Hollywood house and it is ready to sell. As a matter of fact, I think it has already sold to a prominent lawyer in Hollywood. So, we are going to stay out here and help you. We have taken rooms in the Villa and settled in. None of us have much experience with children, but Nicholas said he wanted to keep his staff and not let us go. A few people didn't come, but most of us decided to give it a try."

Liana reached out and hugged her and thanked her and everybody else and invited them in. Jessie was surprised to see this shabby place, mostly because, she couldn't even imagine Nicholas living here. She had known him since he was a child and he had always had a very high standard of living. She secretly thought it was very good for him to see how ordinary people lived.

Kim and Mike and Nicholas came in at the same time. Kim and Mike stood there surprised to see these people here. Nicholas explained that this was his staff and he no longer had a need for them in Hollywood and had ask them to come out here and help. He introduced each of them and Kim offered coffee. They all set at the big table and began talking. Jessie took to Kim right away and began asking her what their duties would be in an orphanage. Kim looked at Nicholas wondering what she should say. Nicholas told her they were her staff, whatever needed done they would do. He said they haven't had experience with children before, but he thought they would do quite well. Each one did different things for me he told her. He pointed out two women, Amber and Kitty and said they were his cooks and they could probably cook something up the children would love. Two other women were the housekeepers along with Jessie. The men took care of his autos and the outside areas. He pointed out Aaron and said he was his driver.

"At your service dear lady," Aaron said.

They all laughed and then Kim told them that she had never had this kind of help. She said most of their help were the older girls and boys. Then she added that she was very glad to have them and she hoped they could all be friends and band together as a team to help these children.

"You mean you have taken care of all these children by yourselves?" A young man named Andy asked.

"Yes, for nearly ten years now." Kim answered.

"Well, if you can do it by yourselves, I suppose I should be able to do part of it."

They all agreed and told Kim and Mike they were very happy to be here.

"You might want to wait and see how things go before you say that," Mike said jokingly.

They all laughed and one after another asked Kim what she would like them to do. She asked them to go into each one the children's rooms and help each child pack their belongings and to put their name on their things. She also told them to keep one outfit out for them to wear tomorrow. Kim showed them where the rooms were and they all started knocking on doors.

Kim turned and looked at Nicholas, "You are a Saint."

Liana cleared her throat jokingly, then she said, "Are you really selling your Hollywood house?"

He looked at her, "What do I need that for? I no longer intend to squander my money on useless luxuries. I am a new man in Christ and I intend to live my life the way He wants me to."

8

WEDNESDAY CAME AND they started their move. Nicholas wouldn't let them go see the place until they moved, he wanted to surprise them. At the Villa Nicholas had them all line up and follow him through the place. It was a very long line and everybody was talking and laughing. When they went inside the talking turned into sounds of admiration.

The kitchen had big walk-in refrigerators and freezers, four ovens, two sinks, three big stove tops and lots of cabinet space, a commercial dishwasher and an island in the middle of the floor with lots of counter space. On one side was a table that would seat ten, this would be for the staffs convenience. The dining room had eight tables that seated ten each. Some of the kids were counting the tables, one of them figured it out and said that eighty people could eat in there.

The living room was filled with overstuffed chairs and sofas. And next to it was a game room with lots of tables and games, it also had book shelves lining the walls.

As they walked down the corridor on the south end, Nicholas told them the youngest children would be sleeping at this end, there were four beds to each room. He told them their rooms had already been chosen for them and their belongings were already there. When they got to the north end he told them this was the where the older children would stay and they would be able to choose their room. There were two beds to each room.

The teenagers were very excited, they looked through each room and found the one they wanted and chose their roommate.

At the end of the south corridor were many more bedrooms for the staff. The master bedroom was at the other end for Kim and Mike plus four more bedrooms, of which, two would be Nicholas's and Liana's.

Liana went into her bedroom, Nicholas was behind her. It was beautiful, it had peach colored carpet and a delightful big white four poster bed with a lovely white dresser and mirror, the closet was a huge walk-in. An exquisite picture of their island was on the wall.

"Do you like it?" Nicholas questioned.

"Yes, it is very charming, I've never stayed in a place this gorgeous before. Is that picture our island?"

"Yes I had it painted for you."

She hugged him and said, I can't believe it, it looks exactly like our island. The waterfall and the cave, whoever painted it must have seen it."

They did, they were flown out there in a helicopter."

"It's perfect, I shall always cherish it."

"Do you like the colors in the room? I picked them for you?"

"The colors are stunning, thank you, but I thought you weren't going to squander your money on useless luxuries."

"I want this to be the finest orphanage money can buy, these children need a nice place to grow up in, and you my dear, I want to pamper always."

"I'm so glad you found God Nicholas, you have become a gallant knight in shining armor, and it fits you."

He laughed, "I won't try to change your mind about that, I like you thinking of me in that way."

"Liana," He said, "When everybody is settled, I want to take you to Aruba, it's only a few miles off the coast, it's the wind surfing capitol of the world, the trade winds blow through the island and it's perfect for wind surfing. I think you will like it and I want some special time with you before I go back to finish the movie."

"When are you leaving?"

"In only three days, we've put a lot of money into the film, more than most. Robert still thinks it won't sell, but you showed me the true meaning of love and I think it will be a blockbuster."

Then he asked, "Will you go to Aruba with me?"

"Is this a date?"

"Yes, absolutely!"

"Then I will go."

The next day they drove to the boat docks and boarded a ship for the trip across the Caribbean Sea to Aruba. When the ship docked, there was a limousine waiting for them, the driver was holding a sign that said Reeves on it. The driver took them to the Grand Hotel, they got their bags, they didn't have much just a change of clothes and swim suit. The driver came around and opened the door and they walked into a marvelous lobby.

Nicholas had gotten them two rooms beside each other he asked her if she wanted to eat now or wait till they got to the beach and get something there. She said she couldn't wait to see the surfers.

"In that case," he said, "We better go get our suits on."

They went to their rooms and changed, he knocked on her door and was standing there with two big beach towels. He had his suit on with a t-shirt and she had a pretty swim suit cover on that went to her knees with sandals.

The limo was waiting for them. At the beach, Liana couldn't believe her eyes, there were people on surfboards with sails as far as the eye could see. Nichols took her to the area where you could rent a surfboard, they each picked one and then found a place on the beach to put their towels and shirts and sandals. When they got to the water's edge Nicholas taught her how to wind surf. She was a natural, he asked her if there was anything that she was bad at and she said she didn't know, she hadn't done everything yet.

They spent a fantastic day wind surfing and after they got back to the hotel they dressed for dinner. A maid came into her room and asked if she needed anything, Liana asked her to button the back of her dress. While the maid buttoned her, she asked Liana where she was from. Liana told her she was visiting Venezuela.

The maid hesitated for a minute and then said, "You must be very careful there."

Liana asked, "Why."

The maid proceeded to tell her of the girls that have gone missing there and of the children that have been stolen. She and other maids had moved to Aruba because they were afraid their children would be stolen. Then she told Liana that sometimes the children are found with parts of their bodies missing, that someone was taking the organs and selling them to rich people who needed them.

"You must be very careful," she told Liana. "You are very pretty and they could kidnap you."

"I believe you and I will be careful, we have an orphanage in Venezuela and have found a child that had been stolen and he has an eye and kidney missing."

The maid shivered and said, "That is why we have moved here it is too dangerous in Venezuela.

Nicholas knocked on the door and escorted her down to the dining room. On the way down Liana told him what the maid had said.

"Liana, I really want you to come back home, I will worry about you here."

"I'll be okay, maybe I'll just stay until you finish the movie and I know everything is all right here."

"Then I shall hire a bodyguard for you and the girls at the orphanage and Kim, she is a very pretty woman also. I will need to hire a new driver to, because I am taking Aaron with me. One of the men at the American Embassy said he would recommend them for me."

At the table he talked about the orphanage and all the plans he had to help the children. She was looking at him with a funny look on her face.

"What's the funny look for?"

"Oh, was it a funny look?" She smiled, "While you were talking about all the plans you have for the children, I was thinking about what an amazing person you are. Here you are, the most famous man in the world practically, sitting at a table with a girl that has really done nothing in her life. You do know that you could be with anybody, anywhere and you choose to be here with me and taking care of a bunch of kids."

"My life is filled with excitement now, before it was empty, and what do you mean practically the most famous man in the world."

She laughed, "Okay, the most famous man in the world."

"That's better," he smiled.

After dinner they walked in the garden at the hotel.

"Liana I hope you come home as soon as you can. I talked to a man at the American Embassy and he told me some of the same stories the maid talked about of people disappearing from here. He said that many young women were kidnapped and sold as slaves. He said that they kidnap them and drug them so heavily that the girls cannot fight back. And, eventually they end up in another country. He told me about a girl that was kidnapped and had escaped, she was American and was visiting here. A man in South Africa bought her, she was able to escape and some very nice people helped her and got her to the American Embassy. She was a lucky one, but what happened to her ruined her life, she needs a life time of counseling.

"I have never felt threatened or scared of anybody since I've been here." She said.

"I will be hiring a new driver and bodyguard and you must not go anywhere without them."

"Okay, whatever you wish I will do Nicholas, now you have me a little scared." She agreed.

"Good, I want you a little scared and aware of the people around you at all times."

He set on a bench and she set beside him, putting his arm around her, he said, "Good, it is settled then.

He turned and looked at her, "If I were to kiss you right now, what would you do? You can't run to the house where Uncle Mike and Aunt Kim are?"

"Have you forgotten sir that I am advanced in the art of karate?" She grinned.

"I think I'll have to take that chance, I only have tomorrow left to be with you."

"Don't worry," she smiled, "I won't hurt you too bad."

At that he pulled her to him and kissed her, she went limp and kissed back, they kissed for a long time and he started kissing her neck.

Suddenly he stopped, she was laying back on his arm with a dreamy look in her eyes. He said, "Hey, if I'm going to keep you respectable I guess I'm the one that will have to be strong and keep you at arm's length. Believe me I don't want to, but you seem no longer able to resist my advances, I'm going to have to be the strong one for both of us now."

She wanted so badly to tell him she loved him, but was too afraid he might not say it back, instead she said, "Oh, yeah, I can be strong to, but I just wanted to know what it would be like to not resist you."

"And so, how did it feel."

She blushed, "It was okay."

"Just okay?"

"Well, if I put my heart out there and tell you how I really feel, you will probably leave tomorrow and never look back."

A very serious look came into his eyes, "Liana, I want very badly to know how you feel."

"You must tell me first, you are the man and I am only a girl."

"That's not very good reasoning, I asked you first you know, but I'm going to expose my heart and tell you. Liana I have fallen very much in love with you," he said almost in a whisper.

Liana's heart raced, she set there in unbelief and tears started flooding her eyes.

"Well," he looked at her, "Are you going to respond? Liana if I've crossed a line and said something you don't want to hear just tell me. Why are you crying?"

She put her arms around his neck and spoke, "Oh, Nicholas, these are tears of happiness. I love you to."

He held her tight then pushed her back, "Are you sure, you know you once told me your mate would be pure. I'm not that Liana, I have lived a very promiscuous life and I'm certainly not pure."

"Nicholas, your life has changed now, you are God's son and the day you were saved, all those sins were forgiven. You are a new man now and you certainly have turned from sin. You must not judge yourself on the past, but from the day you were saved. If God can forgive you everything, who am I to judge; or you for that matter. You're a Holy Priest now, remember the first book of Peter 2:9. But you are a chosen generation, a royal priesthood, a holy nation, His own special people, that you may proclaim the praises of Him who called you out of darkness and into His marvelous light."

You could tell Nicholas' eyes were about to tear. He didn't want her to see him so he put his arms around her and held her tight until he was able to control himself.

While still holding her he said, "What an amazing life I'm going to have with you and God. I used to think religion was boring, but now I find it exciting and challenging."

After Nicholas flew back to the U.S., they were so busy at the new place, Liana really didn't have a lot of time to think about him. He called her daily and that was what she lived for every day.

The Villa was a very happy place, now that they had all the staff, their workloads were much easier. They had given the old pace to some nuns who were helping the dying. It was for street people or anybody who had no place to go and were dying. Liana had volunteered to set with these poor dying souls one day a week. She read the bible to them and listened to anything they wanted to talk about. Many were saved before they died.

This was a whole new experience for her and it broke her heart to see these people. They were so thankful for this place to help them die in peace. She cried a lot with them. When she would tell Nicholas stories of what happened there, it would break his heart to.

"Liana, I never knew these places existed, there is so much sadness and grief in this world. And, I have been completely unaware of it up until now. I have been going through this life care free and only worrying about myself. You have opened my eyes to so much. It may sound crazy for me to say thank you for showing me all this sadness, but

I do thank you for it. I have found it is so much better to give than receive. I am not the same person you first met, I don't even know who that guy was any more."

One day on her way home the driver turned a different directions then the way he usually went. Liana questioned him and he said he thought it was a shorter. But, after going out of the city, she knew something was wrong.

His name was Raul and he hadn't been working for them long. The other driver had gone back to the United States.

"Where are you going?" She asked.

Her bodyguard told her that she was their prisoner now and she must do as they say.

She grabbed the door and opened it to jump, he came over the seat and pulled her back.

He held her down in the back seat and gave her a shot of something. Liana's body went limp and she was floating through the air. At least that was what it felt like to her. He had given her a drug that made you feel wonderful. She lay there quietly.

"She won't give us any more trouble, to bad she isn't a blonde, we could get more money." The bodyguard said.

"Are you kidding? As beautiful as she is, she will bring more money than any blonde."

When Liana awakened, she was in a room with other girls. She looked around and saw fear in their faces.

"Where are we?"

One girl responded, "We are on a ship, we've been kidnapped." She said as she put her face in her hands and started crying.

When she cried most of the other girls started crying to.

One girl that seemed braver then the others, came over and set down by Liana.

"I've heard of girls being kidnapped and sold as slaves, do you think that is what is happening?"

"That's very possible, I hope not," Liana answered.

Suddenly the door was opened and two men took one of the girls. She was crying hysterically.

"Don't worry we're not going to hurt you we just want some pictures," one of the men said.

They took them out one at a time, when the first girl came back, they asked her what happened.

"They only took my picture and brought me back," she answered.

The girls were relieved and not so scared to go after that.

When they took Liana, the men grabbed her arms, "Please," she said, "I will go peacefully just let go of my arms."

They did, and she went with them to a room that was set up with camera equipment.

An ugly little man with beady eyes smiled and told her to stand in front of the camera. Liana did as she was told.

"This one's a beauty," he said, "To bad we can't keep her for ourselves."

"Smile pretty for the camera now." He added.

She looked at him with disgust.

"Oh, a lively one, why aren't you crying like the other girls," he asked?

"Because, my God is with me and He shall not let you harm me!" She said with no fear.

He got up and came over to her and slapped her hard across the face, "Don't you ever talk to me in that tone of voice."

One of the other men stepped forward and said don't, you're going to mar her face, you know we are not to lay a hand on them"

She glared at him, "You will regret that."

The other man grabbed him to keep him from hitting her again, "Get her picture taken and get her out of here."

When she went back in the room with the other girls, they saw her face and one of them said, "Did they hurt you?"

"Yes, but not as bad as the Lord is going to hurt them. My God is a vengeful God when one of his is being harmed. Are any of you girls Christians?"

Several of them held their hands up, "Then keep your faith in God through this whole experience, He is your only hope. And He will help you. No matter how bad it seems just remember He is there beside you."

One of the girls could tell that some of them didn't understand English so she interpreted as Liana talked.

"Now," Liana said, "Let's hold hands and pray."

She prayed for God to avenge the men who had kidnapped them and for Him to help them get free. She prayed for all their families, that God would be with them through all this.

Then she looked at all of the girls and said, "If any of you here does not know God or the Lord Jesus hold up your hand."

Several held their hands up.

"Do you want to know the Savior?" She Questioned.

They all said yes.

"Then I need to spend the time we are here together teaching all I can, because it will take a miracle from God to save us."

Liana spent the rest of the time they were together teaching them about Jesus. She talked with them for several days, before they were taken from the ship, all the girls who weren't saved had gotten saved.

They thanked Liana and told her they were no longer as afraid as they had been and she told them that whatever happened, the Lord would be with them.

All the girls were taken together to a big house, it looked like they were somewhere in Arabia. The style of buildings made Liana think that.

They were taken into a big room with many beds, there were a few other girls there. After the men left one of the girls already there ran over and began talking to them, she was American.

"Are any of you from America?"

"Yes," answered Liana, "how long have you been here?"

"Two weeks now, but I'm afraid they will be taking me soon, I think they got a buyer for me."

"Can you tell me all you know of what is going on?" Liana asked.

The girl's name was Christy, she started telling them everything she had experienced. She said she knew they sold the girls to very rich men and if they tried to escape they got beaten; for examples to the other girls. She told them she was beaten twice so far and they had to wait till she healed to sell her and that was the reason she was still here.

Liana asked if they ever sold more than one girl to a person. Christy told her that they did, that one man bought ten girls one time. They were told they were going to be in his harem.

"Have any of the girls ever escaped?" Liana asked.

"No, not since I've been here, they have tried, but they always come back and get beaten. Both times I thought they were going to sell me, I did something that caused me to get beat. That way I can stay here. While you are here, they treat you very well, because they want to get a lot of money for you."

That night she talked to the new girls that were there, two of them did not know Jesus so she started teaching them. They understood and wanted Jesus for their Lord and Savior, she led them to salvation and the girls prayed together again, asking God to save them from these evil men. She also prayed that God would keep them safe and unharmed while they were here.

They were kept in the room for several days and were ordered to bathe and wash their hair then some women came in with beautiful dresses and under clothing for them. They were dressed and had their hair done.

Then they were taken to a big room which looked like a theater. They were on stage and the chairs in the audience were all filled with men.

9

WHEN LIANA DID *not come home that night, Kim and Mike were very worried.* They knew she was with the bodyguard and couldn't understand how anything could have happened to her. They knew if she had made other plans, she would have called. They had spoken to the nuns where she had been and they told them that Liana left at about four o'clock in the afternoon.

Finally when she hadn't come home by ten they decided they had to call Nicholas. They never called him, so when he got the call he feared something was wrong.

"Hello, Nicholas, this is Mike."

"Yes," Nicholas said, "What is wrong."

"We hate to tell you this, but Liana hasn't come home yet and she left the nunnery at four o'clock."

"Did the car come back?"

"No, but I think if she had made other plans she would have called us, this is not like her at all."

"No, it isn't, have you done anything yet?"

"No we decided to call you first and see what you thought we should do."

"Why don't you call the police and give them a report and I'll call the American Embassy."

"Okay, we will call the police and get back to you when we are through talking to them."

"Good," Nicholas said, "I'll be waiting for your call."

The thing Nicholas feared most may have happened, he was beyond himself with worry.

It seemed a very long time before Mike called him back, Mike told him that the police took a report and said they would look into it. They said they wouldn't worry too much she'll probably show up sometime tonight or tomorrow. That most of their calls usually turned out to be nothing and the missing person shows up.

Then Mike said, "But, you know that is not our Liana. She would never do this, I think something is wrong."

"I do to, did you tell the police to look for the car she was in and the driver and bodyguard?"

"Yes, they did notify the police force to be looking for the car or the driver or bodyguard. I gave them the men's names and they said they would be looking for them."

Then a terrible thought struck Nicholas, "What if those men I hired are the ones who took her? I would never be able to live with myself if that happened."

"Weren't their names given to you from the American Embassy?"

"Yes, I hope they aren't in on this to, you never know, when there is money to be had people will do terrible things. I'm getting on the first plane out there, we may have to find her ourselves."

"In the meantime, Kim and I can start talking to our Spanish friends and see if they know anything."

"All right, I'll see you tomorrow."

After Nicholas hung up he ordered a plane ticket to Venezuela. Then started calling all the government people he knew. The Governor of California was his very good friend and when Nicholas told him what had happened, the Governor said he would be calling on the Venezuelan president and insist that they find her.

Nicholas' other friends said they would do the same and the president's office in Venezuela got more phone calls that night then they ever had before.

Nicholas called the man he had spoken to at the American Embassy and told him if he had anything to do with her disappearance that Nicholas would make sure he went to prison.

That night, the Venezuelan President had their secret service and all the police in Caracas searching for her. The media got hold of the story and were at the orphanage talking to Kim and Mike, they showed them pictures of her. And, told them about the boy who had his body parts harvested. The reporters were aghast at what they heard. When the story came out in the papers, and on TV the people in Caracas started demonstrating in the streets. The public outcry made the President very angry and he told the police to break up the revelers in any way they needed to get them off the street.

Many people were beaten and the demonstration was put to rest. However, the American reporters there showed it in America and the American people demanded that the President do something about it.

The next day Nicholas saw the demonstration was in full force. He took a cab to the American Embassy and the cab driver had to take back streets to get there. When he got there, they told him that the man he was asking for Richard Clemens had not come to work that day. Nicholas had to go through many channels and make many threats, but finally they gave him the man's address.

The car pulled up to the address and Nicholas went to the door, the door was opened a little so he let himself in. The house was empty except for some trash left behind. His heart sank. Now, he knew this guy was part of the group that had kidnapped Liana.

Nicholas had hired the bodyguard and the driver because Richard had recommended them. He met Kim and Mike at the police department. They talked to the police, Nicholas told them about the man from the American Embassy. They didn't seem to be interested they just wrote down the facts. Nicholas was getting angry because of their indifference.

When he left he vowed to get them all fired. As they walked out the door, they were accosted by a man who said he worked in the detective division and would like a private meeting with them. He put a note in Nicholas' hand and walked away.

Nicholas walked to the car before he read the note in case someone in the police station was watching. It was evident to him that the man did not want anybody in the station see him talk to them.

In the car the note said, I will meet you at the orphanage.

They all felt relief, hoping this man could help them. At the orphanage they arrived before him, they left the gate open so he could drive in.

He arrived shortly after them and Jessie showed him into the living room where they were waiting.

He introduced himself as Cruz Hernandez, Nicholas introduced him to Kim and Mike and they all set down to talk.

"I may be able to help you, but first I must warn you to not trust any of the police and do not give them any more information. They are dishonest men and if you give them information they will be able to block any headway you may make. Do not trust anybody unless I tell you to. I have been working on these kidnappings for a while now and I think I know some of the people involved, but of course, I can't even tell my fellow workers because I do not know who to trust. There is a detective I want you to hire. I know you are very rich and this man is expensive, but he is very smart and will be of great help to you. His name is Carlos Santiago and here is his number."

"Why are you doing this?" Nicholas asked.

"Because I am an honest policeman and I want to help, I have seen too many young girls disappear and I know some of the police are in on it. I want to stop this, but it is very hard when you don't know who to trust."

"Now, go call Carlos and I will be talking to him, I might have some information on who the bodyguard and driver are. The police like to brag and laugh about you hiring the crooks, I talk and laugh with them, but it is only to get information."

Nicholas became very angry, "If it is the last thing I do in my life, I will get Liana back and I will have all these thugs put in prison."

"You must love this girl?"

"Very much, she means everything to me."

"We will do all we can for you, in the meantime, do not talk to anybody but Carlos and me."

Nicholas said they wouldn't and they said their goodnights.

That night, Nicholas called Carlos, he hired him on the spot and they were going to meet early next morning. Nicholas was beside himself, sleep was impossible all he could think about was what was happening to Liana. He knew she was strong and smart, he would have to believe that she was holding her own with the creeps that took her.

Liana was holding her own. When they told her to walk across the stage she told them no. The men trying to get her to walk out there were beside themselves. A tall man came walking back to see what the holdup was. They told him she refused to move.

"Then drag her out there," he said.

Two men grabbed her and started pulling her out on the stage, she turned and kicked one of them between the legs. He fell in pain, then the other one grabbed her by the hair and pulled her on out. The men in the audience were laughing, she looked at them and then turned quickly and kicked the other man, he fell on his knees and the audience roared with laughter.

She stepped up to the front of the stage and looked at them, then said, "My God will smite you all for what you are doing. God is with me and he protects the ones he loves. If you are God's enemy He will deliver you all to hell.

The audience got quiet, they could tell by her voice that she was not afraid.

The audience became very quiet, and she continued, "The Lord Jesus is my Lord and my Savior, He is with me and protects me always. If any of you men buy me be prepared for vengeances from the Lord because He will be very angry at you. All of you who are buying women for slaves are going against a Mighty God that abhors injustice. He is a true and living God and will not let you get away with this."

She turned and walked off the stage. When she got off the stage one of the men she had kicked was standing there, he hit her in the face with his fist and broke her nose.

She was knocked out for a little while, they picked her up and carried her to the car. When she came to, Christy was sitting beside her with a big black eye, Liana had blood running down all over her blouse from her broken nose. They looked at each other and then laughed uncontrollably.

Back at the orphanage, Nicholas had met with Carlos and Carlos told him he was sure that he had found the bodyguard.

"Where is that good for nothing?"

"I found him in a night club and followed him home. I think the two of us should pay him a visit. Hoodlums like him are a dime a dozen and they usually tell all they know if they think they're are in trouble."

"They drove to the house where Carlos thought the bodyguard lived. The detective had his gun out and when the door opened the bodyguard was standing there. Carlos put the gun in his face and told him to let them in."

The bodyguard backed up and Carlos told him to turn around and when he did, Carlos put handcuffs on him.

The bodyguard looked at Nicholas and said, "You got the wrong guy, all I did was ride with them."

"Where did you take her?"

"I only went as far as the shipping docks and they told me to leave."

"That's a lie." Carlos said, sticking the gun in his face, "You were with them when they took her to the ship, now tells us which ship they put her on," he jabbed the gun hard into his neck.

"All right, all right I'll tell you, get the gun out of my neck."

"We took her to a ship going to Arabia, I don't know the name of it, but it was getting ready to pull out when we got there."

"If you are lying to us, we will be back and next time we will shoot you." Carlos said.

"I'm not lying, but you will probably never find her."

They left and headed for the docks. When they got there they found out the name of the ship and where it was going and what day and time it left.

The men took Liana and Christie back to their room.

The girls went to the bathroom and washed their faces. Liana took her blouse off and washed the blood off her neck.

"I know Nicholas is looking for me by now," Liana told Christie as she put a t-shirt on. "We need to stay here as long as we can, because if he finds out which ship we were on then he may be able to find us here."

There was a knock on the door, when Christie opened it a man was standing there. He introduced himself as Dr. Sidhu, he walked over and looked at Liana's nose. He told her to sit down and got some bandages out of his case. He felt of her nose, Liana jerked, it was very tender.

"Well," he said, "It is broken, however, it is not out of place, I'm just going to put this small bandage on it to hold it in place while it heals. Then he looked at Christie and said she would be just fine and that both of their bruises should be gone in a couple of weeks.

After he left Liana said, "Well, at least we have two weeks before they try to sell us again."

Christie started laughing and said, "You should have seen the looks on those men's faces when you were yelling at them. At first they thought you were funny, but then I think they may have gotten a little afraid when you talked about God's vengeance. You may have made some of them think twice before buying a girl. I bet you lost these guys some money today."

They came in the middle of the night and took her. She fought them, but was unable to get away.

"Handcuff her," one man yelled.

The other man pulled her arms back until she was in pain, he handcuffed her and they pulled her out into a van. Liana was dressed only in her nightgown with no shoes. The vehicle drove for several hours and when it came to its destination, they took her inside of what looked like a luxurious palace.

Two women were waiting for her, one could speak English, "You must come with us," she said.

One of the men took the handcuffs off and told Liana that she had better not try to escape because the Prince has very fierce dogs guarding the place.

Liana went with the women, they took her to a very lavish bedroom with a magnificent bath attached. They left her in the room and locked the door behind them. Liana looked around the two rooms, all the windows had bars, the only way out was the way they came in.

She looked at the big comfortable bed and pulled back the plush covers, she was so tired. It only took a couple of minutes for her to fall asleep.

It was afternoon when the two women came back to the room, Liana was still sleeping.

The English speaking woman said, "You must get bathed and dressed for dinner with Prince Anwar."

"Who is Prince Anwar and what is your names?" Liana asked.

"It doesn't matter," the woman said.

"It matters to me, if you don't tell me what I want to know, I will not bath or get dressed." She said with her arms crossed, showing her stubbornness.

"If you must know, my name is Elaine and we call her Shawna, it's not her real name, but much easier to say."

"And the Prince?"

"He is from a very well-known family here and they own practically everything and everybody around."

"Why am I here?"

"Because you must have pleased him in some way, you are to be a part of his Harem."

"I will not!" Liana said indignantly.

"The Prince usually gets what he wants, now will you please clean up.

"No."

"Then we will bring the eunuchs in to bath you."

"You're kidding they still have eunuchs in there harems? I thought that was only in the past.

"They still do have them and I am about to call them, now do you want to do this the easy way or the hard way."

Liana turned around and went into the bathroom. She ran the water in the big tub and got in. It felt wonderful to her, Elaine and Shawna came in to wash her hair.

"I don't need anybody to wash my hair," Liana protested.

"Well, suit yourself," Elaine said and left the room.

When Liana got out of the tub she dried her hair and put her nightgown back on. When she walked into the bedroom, she couldn't believe her eyes, there were several magnificent gowns spread out on the bed.

"Which one would you like to wear?"

"Oh, honestly, I'm not going to put an evening gown on, don't you have any dresses?"

"No, you must wear a gown."

"Well, I'm not going to."

"Do you want us to get the eunuchs?"

"I don't care, I'm not wearing a gown!" She insisted.

Elaine left and was gone for a while. When she came back she had an armful of very pretty dresses.

"Here, I'm sure you can find one out of all of these."

Liana took the dresses and looked through them, she found a very simple blue dress that had a hem line bout to her ankles. She took it to the bathroom and tried it on, it was a little loose, but looked very nice on her.

She combed her hair and wore it down, it was very long and straight.

The women had brought her an enormous amount of make-up, but she told them she never wore it.

"Are you sure?" Elaine asked. "The Prince is very particular about his women."

"I have never worn it and I do not intend to wear it now."

Elaine didn't argue.

She was taken to a splendid dining area, the table was set for two. Elaine left her there.

She sat there for several minutes before the Prince came in. He walked over to her and put his hand out for her to take. She put her hand in his and he brought it to his lips and kissed it. He seemed very young. Liana didn't miss how very handsome he was.

He introduced himself as Prince Anwar then set at the table with Liana.

Before he could say anything, she said, "Why have you brought me here?" Demanding an answer.

"Please do not be so angry, I was at the theater when you were on stage and I found you very amusing."

"Oh, that's nice," she said, "you found me amusing so you just bought me for fun. Don't you know what you have done is against the law."

"Who's law?"

"The law of every country, there is no country that allows people to be sold as slaves, especially if they have been kidnapped. And, most importantly against God's law."

"This is a common practice here and most women are not angry. Only the Americans do not like it, but after they are here and grow accustom to our ways they seem to be fine. Usually the women are much better off when they come here, living in all this splendor. Why don't you give it a chance and see if you do not like it."

"These fine palaces do not impress me and I would never accept this kind of life, I will kill myself before I let you or any other man lay a hand on me."

"Do you mean no man has ever touched you?"

"That is right and my God already has a mate for me I am waiting for him. And when I marry I will come to my husband untouched and pure."

There was a puzzled look on his face, "I did not know there were any virgins in America. All we see if we watch their movies is complete freedom of sex."

"Not all American are like that, the family I come from are Christians and they hold purity in the highest esteem. We are hardworking, God fearing people."

"How strange, are there a lot of Christians in the United States?"

"Actually a large percent of Americans are Christians. But, not all are as devout as we are. We try to live our lives according to the Bible, which, of course, is God's word."

Suddenly the door opened and several very beautiful women came in to serve their dinner. Each was carrying a plate of food. Liana was very hungry and the food looked awesome. Each woman brought their bowls to each of them and they were served whatever they wanted. Liana took almost everything, when the women left she looked at her plate it was heaping full.

Prince Anwar looked at her plate and then at her with a questioning look on his face, "I'm sorry," she said, "I am hungry and didn't realize I was taking so much." She was very embarrassed.

"You may have all you want, if you are still hungry when you have finished that you may have more." He said.

She didn't miss the amusement in his voice, she blushed. He smiled and told her to enjoy her food.

The food was so good, "I love the sauces you have on your food they are delicious."

"Yes, we have the very best cooks, as we also have the very best of everything, anything you desire is at your disposal."

"What about my freedom?" She asked.

"Why don't you give it some time and enjoy being here, as if it is a vacation and then we shall see about your freedom. I will not hold you forever against your will, but I will keep you here for a while to see if you could ever like it here."

"We have a saying at our house, if you really love something let it go and if it loves you it will come back."

"But, you do not know me or our way of life so if I let you go you would not come back. You are very beautiful and I could easily love you, but if you don't know me, why would you come back, you must get to know me."

"Do all of your wives love you?"

"Yes, I think so."

"If you let them go would they come back?"

"Yes, I think they would."

"How many wives do you have?"

He smiled, "I don't know, I will have to count them someday."

"You really don't know?"

"Of course, I know, I only have eleven wives, some of the Princes' have in the hundreds. I do not want any wives that I cannot be with often. I have chosen each of my wives very carefully. And I love each one of them."

"Didn't the men in your bible have many wives?" He asked, "I know of Solomon who had over nine hundred wives. So why do you think it is wrong for me to have many wives."

"Because, in the bible it tells me that a man is to take a wife and leave his parents and the two shall become one flesh."

"So, do you know who your God has chosen as a mate for you?"

"Yes, and I'm sure he is looking for me right now and when he finds me, he will deal with you, you should let me go."

"Do you love him?"

"Yes."

"He is a very lucky man, I envy him to have the love of such a beautiful woman. Perhaps, after you have been here for a while and get to know me, I will rival him for your hand."

Liana became frustrated and said, "Can I go back to my room now?"

"You have already tired of my company?" This was new to him, most women don't want him to leave.

He became very short with her and told her she may go.

In the room Liana thought about him, she understood why the women liked him, he was a gracious host and very handsome. He didn't wear the robes or turban that she had expected. He was dressed in a nice suit. She was thinking of what he said, that if he would not hold her forever against her will. But, if he let her go she would turn him into the law, so how could he let her go without being caught. Maybe, since he was a Prince he is immune to any laws or maybe he would have her killed or perhaps sell her to someone else. She knew she must not trust him to set her free. She decided that her best chance was to befriend him and keep him at arm's length until she could get away.

10

NICHOLAS AND CARLOS *had boarded a plane to Arabia.* When they landed, they went straight to the port where the ship would be docked. The vessel belonged to a company called Arabian Shipping.

They decided to go straight to the law and talk to the police, if the police here are like those in Venezuela they didn't have much of a chance of finding her.

At the police station they talked to a detective that handle cases such as these.

They explained what all had taken place and the detective seemed to be concerned. He asked them where they were staying.

"We haven't gotten a hotel yet, we came straight to you from the airport." Nicholas stated.

"Why don't you find a place and settle in? Call me when you have done that, because I would like to come talk with you"

After they got settled in, the detective came to their room.

At the door they shook hands and the detective told them just to call him Ty, it was short for his real name which he was sure they couldn't pronounce.

They laughed and Carlos said, "Okay, Ty it is."

Nicholas had rented a suite with two bedrooms a living room and kitchen and there was plenty of room to set and talk.

Ty told them that there had been a few cases of this sort over the last few months and they were never able to find anything. But, since they know which ship she came in on and the date we should be able to track where she was taken. Then he asked them to go with him to the shipping company. Nicholas told him they would be glad to and would like to be involved in this as much as possible.

An Arab was in the office and could speak English. Ty told him that they believed an American girl was taken from Venezuela and brought here on one of their ships.

"I'm certain that you must be mistaken, we only haul freight, not people."

"This girl disappeared three days ago and we have absolute proof that she was put on one of your vessels. We need to search that ship and look for anything that might be useful in finding her."

"What was the name of the ship?"

"The Arabian and the numbers on it were 76373." Carlos told him.

"Well, it looks as though it is still in port, it is dock seven, here I will give you some paperwork that allows you to search the vessel."

It didn't take long for him to print the paperwork out and he handed it to Ty.

The three men left and drove straight to the docks, at number seven they saw the huge ship. Upon boarding Ty gave the paperwork to a deckhand, he took it to the captain. When the Captain arrived, they were surprised to see he was an English man, he asked them what this was about.

"We have an American girl who disappeared from Venezuela three days ago, one of the kidnappers said they put her on this ship."

"I assure you that there was no passengers on my vessel when we came from Venezuela."

"Good, then you won't mind if we search the ship and talk to your men," Ty said.

"We were just getting ready to pull out, we're going back to Venezuela with a load."

"This vessel will not leave the dock until we have searched it and talked with all the hands," Ty said, he took out his detective badge and showed it to the captain.

Ty called the station and told them to send several men to the ship so they could search it thoroughly. They searched late into the night and Ty questioned one hand after another.

Nicholas was deep in the belly of the ship, he found a small room with a bunk in it. He looked it over good and then looked under the bed. He saw something and pulled it out, it was a bracelet of Liana's, he recognized it, he had bought it for her the day they went to Aruba. He searched the room some more but found nothing. His heart was beating fast when he went up the stairs to Ty and Carlos, he showed them the bracelet and told them he had given it to Liana as a gift.

"Good," Ty said, "Now, we have proof that she was brought here on this vessel and we know that somebody who worked on this ship has to know something."

Ty told the Captain that this vessel was to remain in port until they release it, he showed him the bracelet they had as evidence that she was on this ship.

"Impossible," the Captain said."

, it's not impossible," Nicholas said, his words were angry and he grabbed the front of the Captains jacket and continued, "You better not be a part of this, because if you are we will put you away for a very long time." He shoved the Captain back when he let go.

"I assure you sir, I had nothing to do with this and I want the scoundrels caught as much as you do. If I thought someone had been kidnapped and hidden on my ship, I would have made short work of it."

Ty told Nicholas and Carlos that they may as well go back to the hotel, he said it would take several days to interrogate all the men from the ship.

It was just turning dawn, Nicholas and Carlos decided to have some breakfast and go back to the hotel. After breakfast they went to the hotel, they had been up for nearly three days now with only a few naps.

They slept all day and were awakened by a knock on the door. Carlos had the front bedroom so he answered it and found a young man about sixteen standing there.

The boy said, "Are you looking for a kidnapped girl?" He could speak English very well.

"Yes, come in," the boy came in and Carlos told him to set down and wait for him. Carlos knocked on Nicholas door. When he told Nicholas what the boy said, Nicholas got right up put on a robe and came out to talk to the boy.

The boy told them about the theater and how they put the girls on stage to sell them.

"How do you know about this?"

"Because me and a friend sneaked in and hid up in the balcony and watched."

"Was there an American girl with dark hair?"

"Yes, she was very pretty," he smiled and said, "she kicked the men in their privates that were bringing her onto the stage and then went to the center of the stage and told the men in the audience that her God was mighty and he would bring vengeance on any of the them who bought a girl."

Nicholas laughed and said, "I knew she would put up a fight. What happened to her?"

"When she walked off the stage, one of the men who she kicked hit her in the face with his fist and knocked her out. My friend and I had sneaked down behind the curtains while she was telling the audience how her God was her Lord and Savior and He takes care of the ones He loves."

Nicholas eyes glazed with anger, "Can you show me the man who hit her?"

"If he is still around I can."

Nicholas told the boy to wait for them while they got dressed.

The boy showed them where the theater was and it looked closed up.

"There's probably someone here, there usually is," the boy said.

"I think we should get Ty and have him go in with a warrant," Carlos said.

"Maybe you're right, but when we get in there I want this boy to show me which man hit Liana."

They stayed in the car and called Ty, he said it would take him a while to get a warrant. Ty told them to wait there for him and keep watch.

While they were setting there a man came out.

"That's him!" The boy said.

Nicholas told Carlos to follow him and see where he goes. They called Ty and told him they were following the guy. Ty told them to go ahead and follow him and as soon as he got a warrant, he would call them.

They followed him for several blocks and watched him go into an apartment building. Carlos got out and watched where he went. Then came back to the car.

He went into the first apartment on the second floor. They called Ty and told him they saw where he lives and were on their way back to the theater.

Not long after they got back to the theater, Ty showed up with two other officers. They all got out of the cars and walked over to the theater door, it was locked. Ty told Carlos and one of the officers to go around to the back and watch, he gave them a minute and knocked loudly on the big theater door. There was no answer, they went around to the back, Carlos said the door was locked but it looked like an easy open. The door was old and Carlos tried a credit card in the door, it opened right up.

When they went inside, they were back stage, Nicholas looked around and took the stairs that led to the stage and the men followed him. It was dark, Nicholas found some light switches at the top of the stairs and turned them on. The theater lit up, he walked out on the stage and looked around and he saw all the theater seats in front of him. He knew he was seeing what Liana saw that night, except the chairs were filled with men. He went down to the seats and sat in one in the front, looking up he saw what the men saw that night and could imagine Liana going out front and center and telling them that God would get revenge. He halfway smiled thinking about her, then he nearly cried, knowing she was alone and needed his help. He would find her no matter what, he was more determined than ever, he knew he could not live without her.

Liana had her plan and the next time he called her she was more agreeable. He invited her to ride horses with him. Liana was pleased because she had been setting in that room for two days.

At the stables she was amazed, Anwar had the most beautiful Arabian horses she had ever seen. They were the tall black horses with the black kind of curly mains. She walked up to one and it was so tall, the horse put his head down and she rub his cheek.

"That is my horse," Anwar said coming up behind her, "But, if you must have him, I will ride another."

"No, I will ride the one you give me, I have never seen such a beautiful horse and I love him."

"Well, if you love him then you may have him, his name in Dundee, I told you, you may have anything you wish."

"Oh, no I would never take your horse, just bring me mine and we can go."

Anwar told the stable boy to bring her Reye, he brought out an equally beautiful horse very similar to Dundee.

Liana was in awe, "How magnificent, she is beautiful to."

"I'm glad you like her, let me help you on."

She put her foot up in the stirrup and he held her waist helping her to get high enough to put her other leg over the horse. She had on riding pants that the servant had brought her and she was glad they were riding pants because regular jeans would not have given enough for her to get on this tall mount.

They rode for several miles that day and Liana had never had such a smooth ride on a horse before. After riding a while they came to a brook, they got off the horses and allowed them to drink. Liana set on a protruding rock and he sat on one beside her.

"Are all American girls like you?"

"How do you mean?"

"Well, so out spoken, you are so different then the women here. You just say what you want when you want. A woman here would never presume to talk to a man like you do."

"That is because in America, the men respect the women and give them equal rights to talk or say what they want."

"Are you saying we do not respect our women?"

"I'm not saying that, I'm sure you respect your women in your own way here, but Americans do not restrict their women from living their lives the way they please."

"I am fascinated by that, yet I can't imagine a world where women can say and do as they please."

"You say and do as you please don't you?"

"Yes."

"Then why do you think a women cannot have that same right? Do you think we are not as smart as you and can't possibly make it on our own?"

He laughed, "Women have never been as smart as men."

Liana held her tongue, she was getting angry, but didn't think she should show it. If it was Nicholas talking like this she would have argued with him. But, Anwar had been brought up believing this and she thought arguing with him might make him really mad. She knew these men treated women like a lower life form, more like an animal that they owned instead of a human being. She knew she had to keep her head if she was going to outsmart him. So, instead of saying anything she went over to her horse and rubbed the bridge of its nose. The horse seemed to like her.

Changing the subject she said, "I think Reye likes me."

He walked over to her and said, "Not as much as I like you."

Liana blushed, he took one of her hands and kissed it, looking her in the eyes as he did so. She turned her head and asked if they could ride home now.

He stiffened at her rejection, "Yes, we shall ride home now."

They didn't talk all the way home and both of them were very uncomfortable. At the stable he handed the reins to the stable boy and walked away.

Liana was worried, she knew she made him mad and needed to do something. She ran after him and called his name, he turned.

She came up to him and said, "Please, I didn't mean to make you mad, I was embarrassed and didn't know what to say. I'm not used to men kissing me."

Relief showed in his face, he smiled, "I am very sorry I embarrassed you, I will try not to in the future."

He bowed to her and turned and went toward the palace. Liana stood there watching him. She knew she had come close and had to be more careful with him in the future. She wanted to run back and get on Reye and ride away, but she knew she wouldn't make it.

As Anwar walked to his room he was confused. One minute he thought she liked him, but if he made any kind of gestures to her, like kissing her hand she stiffened. Perhaps it was because she had never been with a man. Anwar had never been with a woman that rejected him in any way, he had bought three of his wives and they were happy to be with him. And why wouldn't they be, he gave them anything they wanted. But, that didn't seem to matter to Liana. She was a mystery to him, which made him want her even more.

That night in her room she could only think of Nicholas and wondered if they would ever see each other again. Fear went through her, she went to her bed and got on her knees and started praying, Dear Father God, please let me make it out of here and back home to Nicholas and my family. She prayed for a long time that night and finally got into bed and slept.

Nicholas was laying in his bed wondering the same thing. What if he never found her? He also began to pray, he prayed, of course, for God to save Liana and bring her back to him and before he ended the prayer, he thanked God for being there for him to lean on. He told God he could never get through this alone.

The next morning when Ty called he told them that they were getting nowhere questioning the hands on the ship. He thought it was time to talk to the man who had hit Liana. He took Carlos and Nicholas with him and they went to his apartment. An unshaven man with no shirt came to the door. Ty found out his name was Ishmael.

"Yeah, what do you want?" Ishmael said in broken English.

"We would like to ask you some questions." Ty said as he showed the man his badge.

"Come in gentlemen, what is it you want to ask me?"

Nicholas said, "We want to know what happened to the American girl you hit in the theater the other night."

"I have never hit a girl, I don't know what you are talking about."

"Let me refresh your memory," Nicholas said, "She was a small girl with long black hair and she kicked you and went out in front of the audience and told the men they had better not buy any girls or God would have His vengeance. Does that bring back any memories?"

Then Ty said, "You might as well tell us it will save you a trip to the police station and getting put in jail."

Ishmael knew if he told them, the person who sold the girls would kill him, he thought he was better off in jail. So, he refused to talk and went with the men to jail.

While he was in jail they searched his apartment, it was filthy.

"How could anybody live in such disgusting quarters?" Carlos asked.

Ty picked up a piece of paper with a phone number on it, "this phone number is the only thing I have found of interest." He said.

Before calling it they decided to find out the name of the person it belonged to. They went back to the police station.

11

NEXT MORNING THE *two women came to Liana's room.* They tidied her room and asked if they could do anything for her.

"Why are you doing this, I know you must know that I was kidnapped. How can you stand by and let this happen. I need you to help me get away."

Elaine looked at her and said, "My dear, I was also brought here against my will. I came from a very poor family and they sold me into servitude to Prince Anwar."

"That's even more reason to help me."

"I'm sorry, but I have seen what happens to the girls who try to get away. If they do not conform to the Princes wishes, he sells them to some horrible people who sell them as slaves to very ruthless men, I have even heard he has killed some. You are much better off here, the prince will give you anything if you accept him."

"Surely with your help, I could get away, you could come with me to America and be free."

"I'm sorry, I cannot take that chance." She told Liana as the women left.

Now, Liana knew what would happen, but she was willing to take that chance. She noticed when they went out that she didn't hear the lock click. She went to the door and tried it, it was not locked. She knew Elaine did it on purpose and felt like she now had someone who at least cared a little.

That night she opened the door and quietly walked down the hall, as she went she listened at each door, the rooms were all silent. She peeked into each one. They were all empty except for the last one and it was locked. She listened at the door, she thought she heard movement. Liana crept quietly back to her room.

At the station they discovered the man's name that belonged to the phone number was Hussein. When Ty made the call, he had the phone on speaker so Carlos and Nicholas could hear what was said.

The man who answered did not speak English, Ty talked to him and when he hang up, Ty told them what was said.

"I told him I was Ishmael and needed to talk to him right away, he told me to meet him in the theater, tonight at nine o'clock."

Nicholas and Carlos went back to the hotel and ordered dinner in their room. They met Ty at the theater before nine o'clock that evening. Ty informed them that they had the place staked out all day and there were several men in the theater. Ty had the place surrounded by police. Rather than going into the building and meeting with these men, he thought it would be safer for the police just to rush the theater and arrest them all.

Nicholas and Carlos agreed. Ty gave the order and the police rushed the building, they broke the front door open and the back door at the same time. They were able to arrest them all, nobody got away and nobody got hurt.

At the station, they put each man into separate interrogating rooms and began talking to them. At first no one talked. Finally Ty found a man that was willing to talk, but only if the police gave him immunity and protection. The police agreed.

He said that Hussein and his men bought girls from a man in Venezuela and then sold then to rich men in Arabia. He didn't know the name of the person in Venezuela, but he did know Hussein's boss. It was a man named Adeeb and he lived in a palace with many women. He also told them that Adeeb had many guards around his palace.

Ty and his men decided to attack his palace in the middle of the night. They staked the place out and had the men to watch and see where the guards were stationed. When Ty and the rest of his men arrived he already had a plan. Carlos and Nicholas were to wait in the car.

The police quietly took the guards out one by one and then broke the door in and went in. All the people in the house were sleeping and when the police came in they were completely confused. They took Adeeb and his men to the station. In the house they found several girls that had been kidnapped, they took them to the hotel Nicholas was staying in and let them call their families. Unfortunately none of the girls were Liana and none of the girls had been at the theater that night and they didn't know her.

Liana was to have dinner with Anwar tonight, she was afraid she couldn't keep him at arm's length much longer. The dining room was beautiful as usual and the food was delicious. They talked throughout the meal, mostly him asking her about her life in America. After dinner, they went for a walk in the garden, it was the most beautiful garden she had ever seen.

"Whoever tends this garden must have a green thumb," she said, "It's is magnificent.

"It is very lovely, but not as lovely as you are Liana."

"I have never really thought of myself as pretty, I'm really rather a tomboy, I like camping and fishing and all kinds of outdoor things.

"Really, you like to camp? That is very unusual for a woman."

"Well, I grew up on a ranch as you know and we always do outdoor things year round."

"You are an amazing woman Liana and I have enjoyed this evening with you, would you like to have dinner with me tomorrow evening," he asked cordially.

"I have enjoyed this evening to Anwar and I would be happy to have dinner with you tomorrow."

He smiled, "In that case, I will leave you as I have some business to take care of, then he asked, "May I kiss your hand?"

Liana offered her hand to him and he kissed it and bowed and told her good night.

She was a little worried because of his actions, she knew now after talking to Elaine that he was a ruthless man and he could kill her or sell her at his whim.

Because of the kidnapped girls they found at Adeebs, they were able to press charges against him. He refused to talk and Nicholas was completely frustrated. He knew that Adeeb could tell him where Liana was, he was so close, but so far.

The police continued questioning the guards and the people who were at Adeebs, but to no avail. After a couple of days, Adeeb's lawyer came to talk with Ty and Nicholas. He told them if Adeeb was to find out where the American girl was taken, he would tell them for immunity.

"He doesn't need to find out where Liana is," Nicholas said, "He knows exactly who he sold her to."

"This may be true and it may not be true, but the bottom line is you will get the girl back and he will get immunity."

"We cannot give him immunity," Ty said. "He will be found guilty of kidnapping the girls at his house. But, perhaps we could give him a lesser sentence, if he tells us."

"How much of a lesser sentence?"

"I don't know we will have our attorney Zayd talk to the court."

"Then you can contact me as soon as you have gotten an answer."

"Yes, we will," Ty told him.

The next day, Zayd told Ty that the court would not give him a lesser sentence.

Nicholas had already informed the American Embassy about all that was going on. They told him to wait and see if the police could take care of it and if not then they would step in.

Nicholas decided, since the police were not getting anywhere, that he would go to the American Embassy and talk to them. He told Ty and Carlos what he was going to do. They agreed with him.

"If nothing gets done soon I am going to call the American media and give them this story. I know if I do I will be taking a chance that the guy who has Liana may do something desperate. But, either way, if the police get close or the media, he may get rid of Liana.

The American Embassy had a talk with some of the men in the government of the Arab World and told them that if they didn't give, Adeeb some kind of deal, that the media will be called into this and it could bring an international outcry. The men in the government told the Monarchy of the problem and they decided to give Adeeb Immunity for telling them all he knew. They thought that he could lead them to most of the people involved.

Nicholas was so relieved, he was sure they would find Liana now.

Adeeb told them who he had sold the two American girls to. He told them the other girls name was Christie and the same man bought them both. He gave them Prince Anwar's address and phone number.

A convoy of police cars headed straight for Anwar's palace. Ty, Nicholas and Carlos were in the front car. There was no fight, Anwar gave up graciously. He knew his father could get him out of this, besides he was a Prince and there were different rules for them. The Monarchy may give him a lecture, but that would probably be the worst that would happen.

Nicholas came up to Anwar, "Where is Liana?"

"So, you are the man she is in love with? You are very fortunate to have a woman like her. I have offered her everything she could ever want and she refused me."

"If you've laid a hand on her, I will kill you." Nicholas threatened.

"I would never take a woman who didn't love me"

"Where is she?"

About that time Liana came out of the Palace with a policeman. When she saw Nicholas, she ran to him.

"I knew you would find me," she said crying and laughing at the same time.

She threw her arms around his neck and he hugged her tight, "I would never have given up looking for you Liana, even if it took the rest of my life."

She looked at Anwar and said, "I told you he would find me and at last I can tell you what I think of you. You disgust me and I hope you will learn someday that women are not just something you own."

Anwar bowed to her and left with the policeman.

Ty and Carlos came up and Nicholas introduced them, he told Liana that without these men he would never have found her. Liana shook hands with both and thanked them.

"Did you meet the other American girl that he abducted the same night he abducted you?" Ty asked.

"No, who was she?"

"We were told her name was Christie."

"Oh, no." Liana said.

She grabbed Nicholas hand and ran into the mansion. They went to third floor and Liana went to the locked door she had found that night. It was still locked.

She knocked on it, "Christie," she yelled.

Somebody yelled back, "I'm in here."

Ty and Carlos had followed, Carlos got out his credit card and opened the door.

When Christie saw Liana, she couldn't believe it. The girls hugged and Liana introduced Christie as one of the bravest people she had ever known.

"How did you find me?"

"I've been here this whole time to," Liana explained then she said, "Nicholas found me and then they told me another American girl was here and then I knew it was you. You see one night I got out of my room and came down this hallway looking in the rooms. When I got to your room it was locked. I was afraid to knock because I didn't know who was in there. Now, I find out it was you. I wish I had been braver, maybe then we could have escaped together.

Nicholas got the two girls a room next to his at the hotel, Christie called her family and they were joyous. She told them about meeting Liana and how they fought for their lives, she told them about Liana going on stage and kicking those men and then telling the men in the audience that her God would punish them if they bought a girl. And how they had both been punched and was a mess but they laughed about it, because they didn't think any man would buy them in that shape. She told them about Anwar buying them and Nicholas saving them.

Her family were so happy they laughed through the whole story. Nicholas and Carlos were in the room as she told her family the story.

When she got off the phone, Nicholas said, "You girls are amazing, after all you have been through and you managed to come out of it with a broken nose and black eye," he smiled and said. "It could have been so much worse."

"Not with Liana praying to God, He certainly took care of us, now I hope they can find the other girls that were taken." Christie told him.

Ty assured them that they were hot on the trails of the other girls. He said that Adeeb was telling who bought the other girls and where they were located. He is also telling them who he bought the girls from in Venezuela and giving them everybody's names that have been involved.

Carlos and Nicholas took the girls to dinner and Liana and Christy told them all that had happened to them. It seemed both girls were courted by Anwar and they both said the same thing about trying not to make him mad, yet keeping him at arm's length the entire time. Liana and Christie vowed to be friends forever and to always keep in touch.

After dinner, Nicholas asked Liana to go for a walk. They were in the garden by the pool.

Nicholas never took his arm from around her, they kept hugging as they walked and finally he held her to him and said, "I am never letting you out of my sight again. I really don't want to let you stay at the orphanage when I leave. Besides, they have enough help now, I'm sure Kim and Mike will let you go home for a while."

"Yes," she said, "I don't want to leave you either."

He kissed her softly and then looked into her eyes, "I love you," he said, "And I never want another day to go by without telling you that."

She smiled and said, "I love you to, I'm the happiest girl in the world."

He walked her back to her room and kissed her on the cheek and said good night.

That night, he slept the best he ever had, knowing she was safe, and he thanked God many times for taking care of her.

The next day, Christie flew back to America and Carlos, Nicholas and Liana flew back to Venezuela. Liana was very happy and she was playful and teasing all the way back. Nicholas loved her in this silly mood.

When they got to the orphanage, Liana was happily reunited with her Aunt and Uncle.

At dinner, Kim told them that they had found the people who had kidnapped the little boy that had lost his eye and kidney.

"You're not going to believe who it was," Kim told them, "It was their neighbor, it seems he took the boy to two crooked police officers and they sold him to a doctor who harvested organs on the black-market. They are all safely in jail now and they also saved two more boys at the doctors house."

"I don't understand how people can be so cruel, but I have no doubts that they can be." Liana said with disgust. "I just wish they could have gotten the people who bought the organs. As long as there are people out there who will buy them, they will keep black-marketing them.

In the morning Kim and Mike took them to the airport and they said their goodbyes.

When they arrived at their destination, Liana's family was waiting for them, Nicholas, agent Robert was also waiting. They greeted each other happily and when they were leaving, Nicholas kissed Liana right in front of her family. He told her goodbye and went with Robert.

In the car it was a little silent, finally Liana told them that Nicholas had told her he loved her. The ice was broken and everybody started talking at once. Of course, Bella wanted to know all about their romance, but Alex and her dad were more interested in her kidnapping. She talked all the way home and told them everything that had happened. When she told them she got her nose broken Alex and Dan wanted to get their hands on the man who broke it. She told them that man was in jail and would be for a long time.

At home Liana got back into the swing of things, she worked every day on the ranch and kept her self-busy. Nicholas was still making the movie and the place he was making it was in Arizona. He told her as soon as he could he would come and see her. He called her every night and always told her he loved her, as she did him.

After a couple of weeks Nicholas asked Liana if she would like to come out there for a while and watch him shoot the movie.

"Yes, yes, yes," she said.

He laughed and told her he would let her know that night what flight.

The first day she was there he took her to the movie site. It was in a small town and the agency that found the place for them had rented a big house for them to live in while they were there. They had turned all the rooms except the living room and kitchen into sleeping quarters. Nicholas' room was on second floor and they put Liana into the room next to his.

At the site she watched them as they shot the movie, 'Nicholas was so handsome' she thought. The woman that was in the movie with him, her name was Julie, was very pretty. Liana couldn't help but be a little jealous when she saw them work together.

When they were finished for the day Nicholas and Julie came over, he introduced them and then took Liana's hand and walked her to the car. That night, they all had dinner together in the big kitchen.

Liana, complemented the cook and Julie said, "Oh, Nicky always gets us the best cook, he gets us the best of everything, don't you darling."

"Well, I try to make life as comfortable as possible under the circumstances."

Liana didn't miss the Nicky and the darling that Julie called him.

Later that evening they were setting in the living room, Nicholas was in an arm chair and Julie came in and set on his lap and started kissing him on the ear.

He pushed Julie up and stood up himself.

"Julie quit it," he said in an irritated voice.

Liana was shocked she could tell that they were very familiar with each other. She got up and excused herself. In the room the tears spilled out of her eyes, she was totally heartbroken. She lay on the bed with her back to the door and sobbed.

He knocked on her door, she didn't answer, he knocked again and she told him to go away. He opened the door and saw her laying on the bed with her back to him, "Please Liana let me talk to you."

She lay there silent and then said, "Do you love her."

"No," he said, "I never loved her we have just played in a lot of movies together and I will admit that we did date for a while, but I never loved her."

"I think she loves you." Liana said.

"Before you came I told her you were coming, I think she did that on purpose."

"I have told her that I am a Christian now and I plan on living my life the way God wants me to. Listen Liana, I knew we would have to cross this bridge someday and I want you to know that my past life was not good. In fact, I am ashamed of it and want only to make up for the way I lived. I know being with someone like me will be hard for you. The movies I made I am not proud of, they were very bad. I hope you never see any of them. I know you don't have any idea of the life I've lived. But, it was pretty worthless. I never want to hurt you and being with me could hurt you someday. You were meant to be with a true man of God, a man that has always lived his life for God. Up until now, that's not me, but from the day I got saved on, I hope it is me. I'm going to do everything I can to make it that way."

She lay there quietly listening.

"Like I said, being with me will be hard for a girl like you and if you think you can't live with my past then I would rather leave than hurt you, I can't bear to see you hurt like this. If you want me to get out of your life, just say the word and I will never bother you again."

"Oh, Nicholas, I don't want you out of my life, I don't think I could live without you now." She said as she set up, her face was a mess it was totally wet with tears and her eyes were bloodshot.

Nicholas took some tissues off the night stand and handed them to her.

He sat on the side of the bed and pulled her to him. He brushed the hair out of her face and looked at her.

She looked at him and said, "You broke my heart Nicholas. You must never do that again, I have never in my life felt like this."

He hugged her and kissed her on top of the head, "I'm so sorry, I'll have to steer clear of all women from now on except you," he smiled.

"You're so handsome and I know women will be flirting with you all the time."

"I shall not notice any of them except you, you will flirt with me won't you."

"Why sir, of course, I will."

They laughed and then he lay on the bed, pulling her down with him, he lay there with her in his arm and asked, "Are you sure everything is okay?"

"Yes."

He turned on his side and looked at her, "I adore you and I don't know how I got so lucky to get you."

"I think if we hadn't gotten stuck on that island together you probably would never have given me a second glance." Liana told him.

"Maybe not, I only looked at sexy, glamorous, made up women and I wouldn't have noticed a true beauty back then. I thank God for the earthquake."

He pulled her close and kissed her quite passionately, then he got off the bed and told her good night.

Next morning when Liana opened the door Julie was walking by she looked at Liana and said, "I really don't know what he sees in you."

Liana just smiled and walked on by. She now knew she didn't have to worry about any other woman. She felt very secure with Nicholas.

Nicholas took Liana to the premiere of the movie, they arrived in a Limousine and a crowd was waiting outside the theater to see him. The media was there and wanted to know who the beautiful woman was with him. Then one of the reporters recognized her and said she was the girl that was in the earthquake with Nicholas. By the next morning her picture was plastered all over the newspapers and TV. The captions read that because of his love for Liana, Nicholas had made this movie with Christian values.

When he talked to the reporters, he told them that it was true but, it wasn't just for Liana. He told them that he was a Christian now and planned on making only quality movies that even Christians could watch.

The movie was a great success to Roberts's relief and they started to plan another one. Liana didn't know it but, Nicholas had a playwright to write a script of their earthquake adventure and he was going to ask her to act in it with him.

12

It was Liana's twentieth birthday and Nicholas wanted to get her something very special. She had no idea what it would be. Her mom cooked dinner at the ranch and Nicholas came. After dinner they gave Liana her presents.

Nicholas laughed, she was like a kid so excited about the presents. Her mom got her a lovely robe and her dad got her a new bridle for her horse, Alex gave her a new spear he had found in an antique store and Bella got her a new top. Liana loved all the presents she was showing them off when Nicholas handed her his present. She smiled at him and opened the box, she couldn't believe her eyes, in the box was the Deed to the island.

"Oh, my gosh, I can't believe it," then looking at Nicholas she asked, "Is this what I think it is?"

"If you think it is the Deed to our island than you are correct."

She jumped and went to him and hugged him.

"I can't believe it, I own an island!"

Everybody laughed, she jumped up and down and danced in circles, holding the Deed in her hand, "Oh Nicholas this is the greatest gift."

"I thought you would like it, now I have a question for you."

"What," she asked?

"I've had a movie script made of our earthquake adventure and I would like you to star in it with me."

"I told you before, I don't know how to act."

Her mom and dad laughed, "Oh, Liana you have been acting since you were a little girl." Her mother said.

"Yeah, but that was just play, do you think I can really do it?"

"Certainly, all you have to do is be yourself and I myself, the movie is about us."

"Go on," Alex said. "You'll do great, you do great at everything."

"Yes, just think I shall have a famous movie star sister!" Bella put in.

Liana laughed, "Well, then I must not let my sister down!"

"You won't regret it Liana, I think this story needs to be told, it will show how God worked all throughout the ordeal," Nicholas said.

"You're right and it will also show how a person can get salvation," Liana added.

"That is right, I think you'll be happy you did it, when it is over. But, I want to warn you that acting can become very tiresome."

"But, it will be fun because you will be there in it with me all the time," she smiled.

"I'm sure this will be my favorite movie I have ever made."

Making the movie turned out to be harder than they both thought. In the beginning of the movie they were strangers and it was hard for them to act like strangers. They finally got the hang of it and was able to reenact it as it really happened. They talked a lot about what exactly happened and their own feelings at that time before they fell in love. The movie brought the whole ordeal back to them, the emotions they felt. They remembered the fear of death they had on the raft and how he asked her to pray. And then her prayer of asking God to save Nicholas so he could find salvation. Robert told them that part of the movie was a real tear jerker. He said he cried when he read it.

They went five days a week making the movie, the more they were together the more they fell in love. Most of the movie was made on the island, they flew back and forth everyday by helicopter. There were huge generators put on the island to for the energy they needed and some big white tents with furnishings in them so they could be comfortable while filming.

One day Liana remarked to Nicholas how different the island was now than when they were stranded. She said she liked it better when it was just the two of them and the only thing they had was the clothes on their backs. Nicholas agreed, he said they nearly starved to death and didn't care as long as they were with each other.

"I actually fell in love with you on this island, of course, I thought you didn't like me at all. And, I knew I would never have a chance with you after you shoved me down and told me your mate would be pure like you. You know at that time I thought that God would never accept a sinner like me and I knew you never would. I didn't understand at that time what a forgiving God He is. I really felt damned until you started telling me about the bible. The more I learned the more I had to know. After the way he saved us every time you prayed I knew there had to be something to it. And as you taught me more, the more hope I had of possibly having a chance with you. I was so in love with you for so long before I dared to tell you."

"Oh, Nicholas, I loved you for a very long time to, but I was sure as soon as we were rescued, you would go back to the beautiful women you were used to. I never dreamed you could fall in love with a nobody like me. Every time I would get my hopes up I would chastise myself for thinking such a stupid thing. I knew you couldn't possibly really love a girl like me. But, I knew I would cherish your kiss forever." She admitted smiling.

"I know, the kiss, it was absolutely amazing, I had kissed lots of women, but none were ever like that first kiss with you. It was the most wonderful thing, I never knew I could ever feel that way. I know now it was because I was so in love with you, and had never truly been in love before."

She laughed, "I felt the same way, of course, it was my first kiss and I never dreamed in a million years that a kiss could make you feel that way. That night it was all I could think about, until I finally made myself quit. God knew exactly what He was doing when he made that earthquake. He knew you would be saved and we would fall in love and He even knew how you would help the orphans. You know the verse that says, I have a plan for you, a plan for good and not of evil, to give you a future and a hope?"

"Yes," he said, "I see where you are going, everything that happened to us was His plan. God is awesome, I love Him so much."

She smiled, "All I can say is it is the best plan I have ever heard of. It gave me the love of my life."

"And I mine," he agreed.

Nicholas decided to buy a house near Santa Cruz since the movie was being made in that area and he would be closer to where Liana lived. The new ranch that Liana's parents bought was only five miles out of town.

He asked Liana if she would help him find a place, he was tired of living in hotels. She was happy to, to her it meant spending more time with him. He was true to his word and had remained a complete gentleman at all times with Liana. Sometimes she wondered if everything was good between them because he never tried to kiss her any more, except a kiss on the cheek. But, he did hold her hand all the time.

They found several houses, he said he needed one with a pool so he could exercise. They finally got it down to two houses. They both had an inside pool and stables. He told Liana he couldn't choose and asked her to pick one.

"I can't pick your house," she said.

"Why not?"

"Well, what if I pick the one you don't want."

"Liana I assure you I love both houses, either will do, now you pick it.'

She picked the smaller one with only four bedrooms it was exquisite she told him.

"I agree," he said. "Then it is settled, now, would it be asking too much to have you pick the furniture and decorations? I would like very much to have a woman's touch for a change. I usually hire it done and they always make it very masculine. I don't think I've ever had a place that looked like a home, most of my places were bachelor pads."

"Do you care if I get my mom and Bella to help?"

"Of course not, I would love if they helped."

He had been picking her up every day and taking her home when they quit working on the movie. He usually stayed and had dinner and while the women did dishes he and Alex played video games together. Or sometimes he would ask Dan some biblical questions and they sat in the library and talked. He had learned a lot from Dan, he was hungry to learn all he could and Dan really liked that about him.

That night at dinner, Liana told them about the beautiful house Nicholas bought. She told them that he wanted her to furnish it and she asked her mom and Bella if they would help. They both smiled and said they would love to.

"Good, then it is settled," Nicholas said then he added, "Listen, I am going to have to leave right after dinner tonight I hate to, but there are some things I need to get done."

When they finished the meal he thanked them and Liana walked him to the door.

Outside, he looked at her then took her in his arms and kissed her, when he let her go she felt dizzy.

"I'm sorry, I just couldn't help myself, I've been trying to keep you at arm's length, but it is getting harder and harder."

"I don't mind if you kiss me sometimes," Liana said.

"Liana, you have no idea of how hard it is for a man to hold back his love with the woman he loves. I love you so much, I want everything to be right between us."

"Everything is perfect between us, I am so happy just to be with you."

He smiled as if smiling at a child, he took her hands and kissed her on the forehead.

"I've got to go, I love you Liana."

"I love you to," she said.

Next morning he called her and said they were taking the day off from the movie. And, he wanted her and her mother and Bella to meet him at the house he was buying.

"I'll give you my credit card and you can go shopping for the house, I especially need a bed to sleep in even if you don't get anything else. I'm closing the deal today while you girls shop."

They met him and he took them in so Emily and Bella could see the house. They both admired the house and told him so.

"Well, I have Liana to thank for it, she picked it out."

"She did a very good job," Emily said.

"Now that you've seen the house," he said, "It will give you an idea of how to furnish it. And don't worry if I like it or not, I'm sure I will love anything you pick. As I told Liana, I always hire a company to furnish my places and I would really like a place that looked like a home for a change, instead of a museum. I love your house Emily it is so warm and feels like home."

"Thank you, Nicholas, we will do our best to decorate this house."

"There is no limit on those cards, do not worry about how much you spend, just get what suits you."

"A woman's dream, no limit on a credit card!" Emily said.

They all laughed and Nicholas told them he would see them later.

"Let's furnish the bedroom first," Liana said.

They drove to the furniture stores and looked at everything writing down what they liked at each store. They decided to stop for brunch and look over their list and maybe pick some things out.

Liana started trying to figure out what he would like when her mother said, "Liana, I think he wants you to pick the things you like."

"Why would you think that?"

"Because I think he is buying this home for you someday."

'Wow, mom do you think he is going to ask her to marry him?" Bella asked.

Her mother smiled and nodded her head.

Liana was taken aback, "You mean you think he wants me to decorate it for us? That he might ask me to marry him?"

"Well, why else would he want you to pick the house and the furniture?"

Liana's face turned red, she hadn't seen it.

"Oh my, do you really think that?"

"Well, I couldn't say for sure, but it seems that way to me, I guess I could be wrong." Emily said.

Liana's heart was beating like crazy, "Oh, mom, I love him so much, I hope you are right."

"Now, perhaps you will look at buying this stuff in a different way, which of these bedroom suits do you like Liana," Her mother said smiling.

Liana smiled and started picking furniture, everything she picked was approved by Bella and Emily. Before the day was out she had furnished the entire house. She told the furniture stores she would call them when they needed it moved to the house.

That night, Nicholas could not believe she had actually found furniture for the whole house, "I am amazed, you don't fool around when you see something you like you buy it," he said smiling at her.

"You told me to pick what I liked so I did, I hope you like it. I still have to choose some wall decorations and a few other things, but no hurry for that, you will be able to live there as soon as they move the furniture in."

"Can you call them tomorrow? I finished the paperwork today and the house is mine. If you will call them tomorrow and go over there to show them where you want everything, I would appreciate it. I still have some other things to do tomorrow and won't have time."

"I would love to, I can't wait to see what it looks like. By the way we picked some blinds to have hung throughout the house the draperies can wait, but I don't think you want neighbors watching you through the windows."

He laughed, "Now, how do you know, maybe I would like that." He teased.

They started saying silly stuff to each other and laughing, Alex came in and joined them. Soon the whole family was in on it, that evening Nicholas had more fun than he ever had. He loved the Baugh's and knew their life together would be good.

The next day Liana called the furniture companies early and had them there and gone by noon. She and Bella went to buy sheets and towels for Nicholas. The floors were hardwood so they picked some lovely multi colored rugs with peach in them and bought a peach bedspread and drapes to match. The furniture was a dark wood and it looked lovely with the peach color. By the time Nicholas came in they had his bedroom finished. He was astonished and he thought it was the best looking bedroom he ever had.

"Honestly, you're not just saying that to be nice are you?" Liana asked.

"No, I truly love it and will love sleeping in here, knowing your hands did this for me."

"Ah, he's so sweet to you Liana." Bella said, "I hope someday I will find a Prince Charming like him."

"I have no doubt you will Bella," he said.

He told them he wouldn't be there for dinner tonight that he needed to gather up his belongings and get them moved in. Liana offered to help him but he told her she had done enough for the day. He said she should go home and relax then he reminded her that tomorrow was Sunday and he would pick her up for church.

He hugged her and kissed her on top of the head and told them goodnight.

He went to the hotel and boxed up all his papers and books and toiletries and gathered up all his clothing. Then he called the bell boy and had him take them to his car. At the house he unpacked everything and put everything in its place. He really did love his bedroom, he couldn't believe Liana could get all this done in just two days. The house was quiet and empty sounding. He couldn't wait to ask Liana to marry him, he bought the ring yesterday while she shopped. His plans was to ask her to marry him as soon as the movie was over so they could take a long honeymoon.

He was happy and slept good that night.

The movie took six more months, and they knew it was going to be a good movie. When it was finished Robert said he thought it was the best movie ever and would be a classic like Gone with the Wind.

The night of the premiere, Liana wore an evening gown and Nicholas wore a tux. They arrived at the theater in a limousine, the white picket fence ran along the sidewalk so fans could not get close to them. They went into the theater and found Liana's family waiting for them, they had invited their church members and the theater was full. There were many other actors there, Nicholas knew them all and introduced Liana to them. The reporters had taken hundreds of pictures of them, they knew this was going to be the biggest event of the year.

When the movie began the theater became very quiet many times during the movie you could hear laughter and at other times you could hear sniffling from crying. All eyes were glued to the screen, even the actors were mesmerized by the film. When it was over, people came to shake hands with them and told them it was the best movie they had ever seen. Even the actors shook hands with Nicholas and told him they thought this would be the biggest hit of all times.

Nicholas told them that it was a completely true story, that they had made this movie exactly how everything really happened. And to some of them he said it was the best thing that had ever happened to him.

Robert was standing by him and he couldn't believe that the other actors had said it would be the biggest hit of all times. He was ecstatic about it.

The church people loved it and called all their friends and told them they had to go see it, that it really showed how God works. They told their friends if they have any doubts about if God is still working in people's lives today that they needed to see this movie.

All the film critics gave it great ratings and on its first day, it brought in more money than any other movie ever had. After the movie came out, the news media really treated Liana with more respect than they had anybody before. Nicholas and Liana decided to put the scene in it where he tried to kiss her and she shoved him down. A lot of young girls who watched the movie learned that it was okay to make a man respect you and turn their advances away.

Liana told Nicholas that God had blessed them and they needed to do the right thing with that money. Nicholas agreed with her and told her together they would figure it out.

13

A WEEK AFTER the opening of the movie Nicholas decided it was time to propose to her. Sometimes he would get worried that she might turn him down. He knew if she did it would ruin his life forever. He prayed about it a lot, he hated having doubts of whether or not she would marry him. He wished he had some way of knowing for sure, but they never talked about it and he thought that was how it ought to be until he proposed.

The day Nicholas proposed to her, he took her sailing, they had gone sailing many times and she was a quick study. She was able to sail it herself if she ever needed to. They were setting still in the water with the anchor down and sails down. They had been swimming and was drying off.

"Liana I think I shall marry you someday, would you be opposed to marrying a rake like me?"

She was surprised and quit drying her hair and said, "Certainly not, you know the woman takes the beast out of a man and you certainly need that." She teased, but her heart was racing.

"Then I shall propose." He said going down on one knee.

Liana didn't know if he was joking or not she stood there dumbfounded.

He had gotten the ring when he was drying, it was in his hand, when she saw the ring she knew it was for real.

"Liana Baugh will you marry me?"

She stood there speechless, tears were coming to her eyes and he said, "This boat is hurting my knee Liana, I need an answer."

She laughed said, "Yes, a million times yes."

He stood up and put the ring on her, it was a magnificent ring.

She threw her arms around him and said, "This is the happiest I've ever been."

He kissed her lips then the side of her face, he whispered in her ear, "Liana I love you so much, I can't wait until you are my wife." They parted and looked at each other.

She had a funny look on her face.

"What's wrong?" He asked.

She said, "I'm a little afraid, I don't know much about love making and I don't know if I will do it right."

He laughed and said, "Liana you are going to be the perfect wife, I shall cherish you always and when we are old we will have great memories."

That night at Liana's house she showed everybody her ring, as she showed it to her mother, Liana said, "You were right mom."

"Of course, I was right, Nicholas had already asked your dad for you hand, so I kind of knew."

Her mom told everybody what Liana was talking about and they all laughed.

The wedding date was set for only a month away. Nicholas and Liana wanted to travel to several third world countries after the honeymoon and find a place in each country to start an orphanage. They knew if Venezuela was like it is that many more countries may be in more need. They knew for sure they were going to Bolivia and Ethiopia, possibly Haiti and South Africa. Nicholas planned to be with Liana the whole time so nothing like Venezuela could happen to her again.

Because of Kim and Mikes expertise in starting the orphanage, Nicholas asked them if they would travel to the places they found that needed orphanages and get them started. He told them they would never have to worry about expenses, the charity organization he and Liana was starting would take care of that. They would have to find a building, furnish it and hire someone trustworthy to manage it. Then stay long enough to see that it was under good management. Then after they set them up they could oversee them, traveling from country to country whenever they wished. Kim and Mike were excited and said they would love to and that they were so thankful that he and Liana would be helping the children.

The wedding would not be to lavish. Liana refused to spend too much on it.

She told Nicholas that it was foolish to spend too much money on it, he laughed and said, "But Liana I don't think you understand how much money we have, we have enough to last several lifetimes. The movie we made was the biggest box office hit in history, it made more money than any movie has ever made."

"I do know that, but when I think of the starving children and all the poverty I can't stand to splurge a lot of money on anything."

"I love you for that Liana, most women would be going crazy buying everything. You are one of a kind and best of all you're mine."

They had become much more comfortable with each other since the engagement. Any time they were together, he was either holding her hand or had his arm around her, they never tired of each other.

One day she asked him, "Do you think we will ever be indifferent to each other, I know mom and dad were very much in love. But, they never hold hands or show each other much affection. And I do know that they still love each other."

He answered, "I suppose eventually the fascination that each of us have for the other will wear off and we will be comfortable just being together. But, I'm sure I will always be aware of your presence."

"As I will yours." She stated.

"I think our life together will be very interesting, we shall make many more movies together and be witnesses to God through them."

"You want me to make more movies?"

"Yes, you're the best actor I have ever worked with and I will not make another one unless you are in it."

"You really think I am the best actor."

"Absolutely!"

"It will be a wonderful life, we shall make movies and travel to the orphanages and perhaps have children of our own someday." She said.

"We've never talked about children, I think I would love to have a little Liana running around the house. That's strange because I've never wanted children until I met you."

"Perhaps we will have a little Nicholas running around."

"Oh no, two of us, that would be too much." He said teasingly.

"You could be right," she agreed teasing back.

Liana, Bella and her mom were planning the wedding and had been very busy getting everything ready for it. The invitations were sent out as quickly as possible. And they worked day and evening getting things ready.

Two weeks before the wedding Liana had gone shopping for a few things she still needed. She had parked behind the store in a parking lot. There was a van parked next to her car and she could barely get between them to open her door. She hit the unlock button on her keys and as she reached for the door handle, the side door of the van opened and somebody grabbed her from behind and pulled her into the van. It happened so quickly that she didn't have a chance to fight back.

"Who are you and what do you think you are doing?"

She no more got the words out of her mouth when he stuck a needle into her arm. In a moment Liana was totally out.

When she awoke she was in a room handcuffed to a bed with a scarf tied around her mouth. She hadn't been awake long when the door opened. An ugly little man came in, she recognized him as a man she had seen on the ship when she was abducted to Arabia. She wanted to yell at him, but her mouth was gagged to tightly.

"I am here to take you to Prince Anwar again and this time you will not get away. He has never forgiven you for leaving him and is paying me more to get you then he has ever paid me before. He has been watching you and knows you are about to be married. He said he would marry you before Nicholas did and he would have you as a wife. Don't give me any trouble, because I have permission to beat you if I have to. I'll be back soon to take you to the ship."

He left and she was very afraid this time, she knew if Anwar would go to these lengths that he was crazy. He must have been stalking her somehow. She tried to get her hands out of the handcuffs but they would not slip through. She pulled so hard on her hands that they started bleeding. She hoped the blood would be slick enough to help her slip her hands out, but the cuffs were too tight.

That night she was taken to a ship and put in a very lavish stateroom. They handcuffed her once again to the bed and kept the gag in her mouth. She wondered why she wasn't taken below decks. She was helpless, she could only set there while the ship pulled out of the dock. After being on the water for a while, Prince Anwar came into the room. He walked over and took the gag out of her mouth.

"I'm very sorry about the way they have treated you."

"Why are you doing this are you crazy, you should know you cannot get away with this."

"Oh, but I can, because they will never find you. You see I have obtained a new residence in another country that nobody knows I own, they will never find you."

"I will spend my life trying to get away from you, you will have to keep me locked up at all times. I will never love you."

"Well, time will tell about that." He looked at her wrists, "Oh dear, I will send doctor Sidhu to look at your wrists. We will be back soon."

When he came back with the doctor, they unlocked the handcuffs and the doctor bandaged her wrists.

"We will leave the handcuffs off now, there is no way out of this room unless you want to jump in the sea out of that portal. I will send your dinner in shortly."

They left her alone, she walked over to the portal and looked out, the sun hadn't started setting and she knew her mom and dad or Nicholas didn't even know she was missing yet. They brought her a tray of food and to her surprise she was hungry and ate.

That night at dinner Emily said, "I don't think Liana should be this late, she only had a few things to get and I'm a little worried."

"Now Emily you know how girls are when they are shopping maybe she just lost track of time."

At ten o'clock, they called Nicholas to see if she was with him.

"No," Nicholas sounded alarmed. "You mean she isn't home yet?"

"We thought she might be with you and didn't want to bother you if she was."

Nicholas told them he was going to call the police and see if there might have been a wreck or something.

Nicholas had a very bad feeling he called the police and they had no information for him. On a whim he called the port authorities and asked if a ship from Arabia, called the

Arabian was docked there. To his surprise they said yes, but it had pulled out several hours ago. Nicholas called Dan and told him he thought that Prince Anwar may have abducted Liana.

"What!"

I know it sounds crazy, but I called the port authorities and they said a ship from Arabia, the Arabian, which was the name of the ship that abducted Liana the first time, was in port."

He told Dan that it had pulled out of port several hours ago, and he had a really bad feeling that Liana was on that ship.

"I'll meet you at the port authorities as quickly as I can." Dan said.

Nicholas got in his car and drove straight to the docks.

Dan showed up shortly after he got there, they went to talk to the authorities in charge. When they finished telling their story, the men were amazed and said as far as they knew nothing like this had ever happened before.

While they were talking, the police called Nicholas and said they had found her car in the parking lot behind the store, her keys were on the ground beside it.

Nicholas had no doubts of what happened after talking to the police. He told the port authorities and asked if there was some way they could stop the Arabian. They said they would call the Coast Guard and have them detain the ship if it wasn't in international waters yet.

The port authorities told the coast guard they thought there was a kidnapped victim on the ship. The coast guard got the directions the ship was going and was going to deploy a helicopter to detain it.

Liana was in the cabin when Anwar knocked on her door.

She answered to door and he said, "It is a beautiful night out Liana would you like to walk on the deck?"

She went aboveboard with him, they walked along the deck.

"Liana I hope you will give me half a chance, I haven't been able to think of anything but you since you left."

"So you spied on me and knew what was going on in my life?"

He took hold of her arms and pinned her against the railing, "Yes, please forgive me, but when I found out you were marrying Nicholas, I would rather have died then let him have you."

He tried to kiss her, she jerked free and said, "Well, I would rather die than be with you."

She ran ahead of him and climbed over the railing.

"Liana what are you doing? If you jump you will die."

She looked down at the water, it was very far, and the moonlight was shining on the waves, it looked dark and dangerous, "You must leave me alone or I will jump."

He ran to her and tried to grab her, she looked in his eyes and said, "I'm not going back to Arabia." She jerked her arms free and fell.

It seemed as though she fell forever, she got herself straightened up so when she went into the water, she went feet first. She sank into the ocean deeper and deeper, by the time she came up she could not have held her breath another second.

The men in the ship got lights and shown them in the water, but it was too dark and they couldn't see much. The ship was moving too fast and Liana lay still in the water as she watched it move away. While they were trying to spot Liana, the radio man told Anwar that the Coast Guard wanted to talk to him. He said to tell them they were having an emergency and he could not talk to them now.

Anwar yelled to the men to turn the ship around and backtrack exactly the way they had come.

Liana floated on her back as she watched the ship go out of sight. She was afraid, but the anger she felt overrode her fear, she started swimming back in the direction they had come from.

She knew it was probably several days for her to make it back, but she was determined.

Anwar took the ship back to the area where she jumped, but he knew they would never find her. He told them to go back out to sea. They hadn't gone far when a helicopter flew overhead, they radioed the ship and told them they were boarding. The crew moved out of the way and gave the helicopter room. An officer from the Coast Guard came over to Anwar and told him since they were not in international waters yet, that he was detaining his vessel.

"Why are you doing that?" Anwar questioned.

"It has been reported that you have a kidnapped victim on board."

Anwar set down and put his head in his hands and said, "She is no longer aboard."

"What did you do with her?"

"I did nothing, she jumped off the ship, we have been trying to find her, but with no luck."

"At what longitude and latitude were you when it happened?"

"The men in the control room can tell you."

Anwar took him to talk to the Captain of his ship. The Captain said he couldn't pinpoint it exactly, but he could get very close. The Coast Guard officer radioed the Coast

Guard Station and told them what happened, Nicholas and Dan were there when he told them that Liana had jumped off the ship. The officer said to send some Coast Guard vessels ASAP so they could start a search.

Then he told the Captain of the ship to go back to the port that he was detaining them until this was cleared up. Anwar told the Captain to head back to Arabia. The Captain refused to listen to Anwar and took the vessel back to port.

Many Coast Guard boats and helicopters were deployed they were headed Liana's way.

Nicholas and Dan were able to get aboard one boat. They were both worried sick and wondering if she even lived through the jump. Nicholas knew how big that ship was, but he knew if anybody could do it, Liana could and he told Dan that.

Liana was floating on her back and taking long easy strokes to reserve her energy. She was praying all along for God to help her. The sky was beautiful there were thousands of stars, she lay looking at heaven and praying to her Father. After a couple of hours the waves became rougher, they started tossing Liana around. The rougher it got the harder it was for her to keep her head above water. Suddenly her leg scraped on something then her head hit something hard, a rock. She was being pushed ashore, she couldn't believe it.

As she scrambled ashore, she kept saying over and over, thank you Lord, thank you Lord. She crawled onto a sandy beach and lay there, she didn't even realize it when she fell asleep.

Nicholas and Dan went back to shore with the boat and when they got there a helicopter was getting ready to go.

They told the pilot who they were and asked if they could ride with them. He told them they could so they hurried into the copter.

It was just becoming dawn when they flew out. The pilot flew to where they thought she had jumped then started a circling pattern. Nicholas and Dan were watching the water, they never took their eyes off it. The circle got bigger and bigger and after about a couple of hours they saw an island off in the distance.

Nicholas watched as flew closer to the island, he couldn't believe it, it was their island. He asked the pilot to fly around the island. As they went over it they were low enough to see the huge generator that had been left there after the movie. Then when they went over the beach, Nicholas saw a small speck on the beach.

"It's Liana," He yelled pointing at the speck that was getting bigger.

Something loud woke Liana up, she set up and saw the helicopter flying towards her. She jumped up waving her hands. The pilot slowed the copter and landed it not far from her. Nicholas jumped out of the copter and ran towards her. She couldn't believe her eyes, it was Nicholas, she ran to him and they embraced.

He held her tight and said, "God has stepped in again and saved you. One of these days you are going to wear God out."

She said, "Nicholas I cannot believe you found me, how can this be?

"I don't know Liana, it seems to be getting easier and easier to find you." They laughed happily.

They walked to the helicopter and Dan was waiting, he hugged Liana and they boarded the copter.

That night at the Baugh's there was a very happy reunion.

Because Anwar was in the United States, he was detained and would stand trial for kidnapping. There was nothing his rich father could do for him this time.

The wedding day finally arrived. Liana was very nervous, Bella and Emily were with her assuring her that it would be fine and she would make a lovely bride.

The church was big, but not big enough, it was completely full and some of the people had to go to the community room and watch it on a big screen.

When Liana walked down the aisle with her dad, he had tears, when Emily, Bella and Alex saw him crying, it made them cry to. Nicholas was not immune either, seeing Dan's face made him feel tears starting to come to his eyes.

Liana was so beautiful, Nicholas couldn't believe this was finally happening, he smiled at her and she smiled back. She was dry eyed and happy. They said their vows to each other and the preacher told them they could kiss. Everybody clapped their hands and laughed while they were kissing.

After the wedding they went to the country club to celebrate. While everybody was having dinner they changed clothes. Liana came in with her flowers and all the girls lined up to catch them. They stayed for a while celebrating with everybody then they announced they were leaving.

Nicholas guided her out the door and everybody was lined up along the sidewalk with rice, they ran to the limo and was gone.

In the car they laughed and talked about how fun it was and when they got to the hotel he carried her across the threshold.

After closing the door he took her in his arms and kissed her the way he had always wanted to. The wedding night was enchanting, Nicholas was so loving he took her fears away and together they learned the pleasures God had given the marriage bed. They belonged to each other now, totally and completely.